# A KIND OF
# KADDISH

# A KIND OF KADDISH

Stories by

Jerry Wilson

Foreword by
J. S. Breukelaar

LEAKY BOOT PRESS

*A Kind of Kaddish*
Stories by Jerry Wilson

*You Don't Live Here* first published in 2013 by
Leaky Boot Press. This expanded edition, retitled
*A Kind of Kaddish*, with three additional stories and
an author's introduction added, first published in
2015 by Leaky Boot Press.

http://www.leakyboot.com

ISBN: 978-1-909849-19-8

# CONTENTS

| | |
|---|---|
| Foreword | 11 |
| Author's Introduction | 15 |
| Gwendolyn | 17 |
| Because the Wind | 29 |
| Burn | 41 |
| Nothing to It | 53 |
| Little Apocalypse | 63 |
| Looking For Nirvana | 73 |
| Birds Are Good Company | 81 |
| The Coconut Chick | 89 |
| A Guy's Gotta Have Friends | 97 |
| The Reality Is | 105 |
| You Don't Live Here | 115 |
| Waiting | 119 |
| Too Late | 129 |
| Hay Is Dreams | 139 |

*Human beings make a strange fauna and flora. From a distance they appear negligible: close up they are apt to appear ugly and malicious. More than anything they need to be surrounded with sufficient space—space even more than time.*

Henry Miller, *Tropic of Cancer*

I remember,
We were flying low,
And hit something in the air.
Bloodrock, D.O.A.

THE STORIES IN THIS COLLECTION ALL take place in and around the parks, cemeteries, and nature preserves in Boise, Idaho, where the author has worked as park ranger. They are loosely structured around a friendship between the park ranger, Dick Swiveller, and Winston 'Franzia' Weatherby, the only wino Swiveller knows who actually drinks wine.

In the opening story three men trudge across the Boise snow to bring a packet of cigarettes to a friend and her baby hiding out from the man who beats her up. Overhead the sun breaks through, 'like a gaping wound.' In "Coconut Chick," the park ranger Dick Swiveller goes to see his social worker after being accused of violating a corpse. In "Nothing to It," he helps Weatherby scrape twin human turds off a barbecue grill.

'Far out man,' they marvel. 'Just like modern art.'

Home is where the art is, yeah. Something like that.

Yet Wilson's skill is to create, in every line, every image, the unnerving sensation of something just over the horizon, something out of frame, partially seen. Bare branches claw the air, 'as if to grab onto immortality;' blue herons soar over the mountains; strains of Elvis the King are carried away on the wind, and Weatherby stares into the dying embers of his fire, as if to affirm the vantage point of the idiot, the savant, the visionary. But that other King, Mr Fisher, has left the building, and those looking for a hooker with a heart of gold, or a Madonna of the squat, please move on, nothing to see here. Instead there's One-eyed Rita, who builds bird cages out of garbage, and the obnoxious trailer preacher Oswald Moody, and the Pastor Billy Roper, whose real estate portfolio comes in handy with the ministry. (And yeah, so there is actually a G.O.D and a Jesus, but that's another story.) The feisty tramp Fern waves her cheap lighter under Swiveller's face and says that she'll use it to light the flames of hell for him while she's sitting in heaven swapping lies with the Lord, because after all, she's a Methodist. Well, Weatherby tells us, unlike the filth who befouled his barbecue grille without leaving any of the usual scraps of toilet paper, at least Luther wiped his ass.

According to the gospel of Winston Weatherby, to whom this collection is dedicated, Luther got religion while parking a squat. So much for piety. Yet there is a stark, almost Calvinistic quality to Wilson's language, as precise and hilarious and subtly incendiary as the people and the landscape it brings to life. Addled eyes float like 'oysters in pool of cocktail sauce.' Lines of blood in a nightmarish mensroom form a raw cuneiform, orgiastic hieroglyphs. A hole, nicknamed Nirvana, cut between the stalls looks like a 'crude mandala or roulette wheel.' In the title story, the erstwhile Fern totters off to get another beer, the shit stains down the seat of her pants 'like a vestigial tail.'

Who lives here?

Like the best collections—one thinks of Bukowski's *Tales of Ordinary Madness*, William Gibson's *Burning Chrome*, Flannery O'Connor comes to mind as do Ambrose Bierce and J. G. Ballard—each story in *You Don't Live Here* reflects on the previous one, distorts and magnifies the one to come, as if to give the lie to the very suggestion that there is anywhere else, any 'there' outside this 'here' of these dens under the boughs, these squats and hideaways and frozen salvage yards, as if the America to which it hazily refers, the world of holiday shoppers and comfortably insured bird watchers and lilac- scented springs and Taco Tuesdays, is a mirage, a ludicrous dream.

Yet perhaps the most significant way in which the title of this collection resonates, is in Wilson's subtle pyrotechnics of reducing the American dream to ashes and then resurrecting it as art. Like a 'Little Apocalypse'—surely one of the most powerful of the stories, when, just our range of vision, the little tramp Nan face plants in the dirt 'as if hearing the call of a far off muezzin.'

Who the hell lives here?

*J. S. Breukelaar*

J. S. Breukelaar is a poet, short story writer and novelist. Her first novel *American Monster* will be published by Lazy Fascist Press in late 2013 or early 2014 and her critically acclaimed short story and poetry collection, INK, was published by Les Éditions du Zaporogue in 2011.

IF NOT FOR A MOB OF DRUNKEN FOOTBALL **fans, I** might never have written the stories in this now expanded collection. One fall day in 2006 I had just spent several hours picking up the considerable amount of trash and debris left in Julia Davis Park by tail-gate parties during one of the Broncos' games. Amongst the scatter of alcohol containers, soiled clothing, broken canopies and chairs, puddles of vomit and what not, I found an unopened box of red Franzia wine.

Remembering I had recently met a guy named Tom who lived under a spruce tree in Quarry View Park who drank that very same brand of wine, I decided to run it over to him. He was happy to receive the wine and offered to show me the improvements he had made on his tree. He'd "done the place up," he said. Naturally, I was curious. Underneath the boughs of the huge spruce, Tom had spread carpeting he scrounged from a neighborhood trash bin, upon which he had his bed roll, a battered night stand and a chair. We immediately became friends and Tom became the inspiration for a character I called "Weatherby."

He also became my first dedicated reader. I was 45 years old and just getting started, yet he treated my early manuscripts like they were Holy Writ, carrying them everywhere in his backpack along with his small collection of favorite books and his cleanest dirty underwear. For the next six years, whenever I had the chance, I steered the city truck towards Quarry View for a little companionship, conversation and a good laugh. Tom always had some funny quote ready from whatever book he'd managed to scrounge out of the "Free" basket on the front stoop of the Good Samaritan Thrift Store, that is, until he was permanently 86ed one day for some sort of drunken altercation with the clerk.

With the addition of three new stories for this updated edition and my resignation from the parks department this past December, this series is now complete.

A word of caution: These stories are not pretty. I pull no punches. My characters are damaged people—crazies, drunks, quitters, failures, bums, and park employees. Nobody attends Alcoholics Anonymous meetings and sobers up; nobody gets a job, buys a house, or sends their kids to college. Certainly no one attends Bronco football game tail-gate parties. For the most part my characters survive day by day, get drunk, laugh a lot and die in their early fifties. Of the dozens of people I befriended during my years working for the parks department, only a handful are still live. And they don't have long.

*Jerry Wilson*
Boise, Idaho
2015

Across the street and down a ways sits Cypress Grove Park, where you'll find grass, trees, a pond, birds and fresh air. To get there, however, you have to pack up all your stuff and haul it with you. Anything left behind is immediately stolen. Being only a stone's throw from the Sanctuary, the dubious shelter of the freeway overpass is more accessible. Besides, everyone knows Cypress Grove Park isn't home.

Under the bridge, Oliver Nubbins adjusted his polyfoam mesh parks department cap and scowled contemptuously at a family asleep on the dirty concrete. Oblivious to the continual rumble of traffic overhead, the woman slept on her side on a large sheet of cardboard cradling a puppy. Her once white trousers had slipped down as she slept, exposing the crack of her ass. Her two toddlers, their hands and faces smeared with oily street grime, slept in their strollers. Above the children's heads, the stroller canopies were piled high with blankets, green tarps, and a dozen or so plastic Walmart bags containing the family's belongings.

"People like that shouldn't be allowed to breed."

Nubbins piously clenched his jaws. He had only two teeth left in his jaws, his lower canines, and since he rarely put his dentures in, he was able to express his disapproval by tucking his chin firmly up under his nose.

GWENDOLYN

"I'd like to see you tell her so." Dick Swiveller laughed. "She'll set your ass straight, Nub. Humble you out in no time."

Nubbins didn't reply. He spat at a discarded beer can and missed.

"The mayor is out of jail."

"I can see that."

Nubbins eyed the group of drunks sitting around their usual rickety table—among them Mayor Tuck, Swann and Madeleine. All the previous night, they'd been hitting Swann's new batch of raisin jack. It was an evil smelling swill, a brownish sludge of canned fruit, raisins, sugar and yeast fermented for a month in two five-gallon water cooler jugs hidden in the shrubs. Only a couple of gallons remained, upon which floated large chunks of mold.

"They'll never change," Nubbins said in disgust. Without doing much, the people that lived under the bridge, particularly the drunks, always managed to get under Nubbins' skin. Besides, he was always grumpy in the mornings. In spite of his nightly regimen of a 12-pack of Milwaukee's Best and a couple milligrams of benzodiazepines, he slept badly if at all.

The two parks department drudges approached the table. Mayor Tuck was holding court, lecturing Swann and Madeleine on the finer points of something or other. At 64, he was the unelected yet official mayor of the drunks. Whether he was mayor because of his longevity and experience or because he happened to have the loudest voice was a matter of dispute. He was wearing a maroon corduroy baseball hat with the name Hensel Phelps embroidered on the front panel.

"Who's Hensel Phelps?" asked Nubbins.

"I don't know. They gave it to me at the jail. Along with this cool shirt." It was a beige hooded sweatshirt with frayed cuffs and the word BONG stenciled on the front.

"Fuck the shirt," said Swiveller. "You had us all worried, you bastard. We didn't think we'd ever see you again."

"That's what I told him," Swann slurred. Tears came to

his bloodshot eyes. Swann sometimes became maudlin when he was drunk.

"I don't know what the hell you all were worried about. I was innocent."

"What difference does that ever make? You're already a convicted felon and you went and got yourself into some seriously deep shit."

Several months before, Mayor Tuck was drinking with Swann and another character, Garland Bilbo, a skinny rat-like man with a huge purple nose, at Bilbo's apartment. The beer supply ran low so Bilbo gave Swann 20 bucks to run to the store for more. When Swann returned the cops were there. Bilbo claimed the mayor had ripped him off, stabbed him and thrown him down the stairs. Since Mayor Tuck was a felon, having spent nearly 20 years of his life in and out of various penitentiaries, the cops believed Bilbo's story. Tuck was booked on two class-A felony counts—aggravated assault with a deadly weapon and armed robbery.

"Well, like I said, I didn't do the crime. That mother-fucker Bilbo didn't even show up to testify at the trial. And he was the star witness. Blew his chance to be in the tabloids, the idiot."

Mayor Tuck laughed and stroked his scraggly beard. His face was battered and scarred, his nose crooked and nearly flattened to one side. Most of his right ear was missing, the mark of a botched suicide attempt. He'd stuck the barrel of a gun under his chin but at such an angle the bullet exited near the top of his mandible, blowing off the ear.

"Crazy Tracy smeared shit all over both of the porta-pot-ties," said Madeleine, motioning towards the portable toilets a stone's throw away. "The last time I took a piss I had to wipe with a Ray Mart receipt."

Madeleine tugged indignantly at the wiry hairs of her sparse chin beard. She wore a long mandala-print skirt and a blouse elaborately embroidered with a motif of Indian men in turbans riding elephants. The pockets of her apron bulged with all her junk. From a belt around her waist hung her water bottle, a pouch, a long hunting knife, and a pair of brightly colored maracas.

"Call the porta-potty company," Nubbins replied. "The number is on the door. We don't service them. How many times to I have to tell you that?"

"How many times do I have to tell you I don't have a fucking phone?"

"Life is hard." Nubbins pulled a blue cleaning rag from his pocket and loudly blew his nose.

Swiveller retrieved several rolls of toilet paper from the city truck and walked over to the portable toilets where he was joined by Nubbins, Madeleine and Mayor Tuck. Swann stayed behind, drinking his jack and smoking a cigarette. He said he wasn't in the right mood for Crazy Tracy's shit.

In the first toilet, smears of shit streaked up and down the walls and over the seat. The stench was appalling.

"Goddamn Crazy Tracy." Madeleine scowled and looked as if she were going to be sick.

Swiveller opened the door to the other toilet. Fly Swatter stood tottering next to the plastic urinal. His trousers still zipped, he held an invisible dick in his hand. A dark shiny wetness spread rapidly down the front of his pants. When finished, he shook off and made the motions of doing up his pants. Retrieving his fly swatter from the shit-streaked seat lid, he whacked at the dozens of flies swarming around his head and walked out.

"I had no idea Fly Swatter was such a great mime artist." Mayor Tuck was obviously impressed.

"Me neither. That was the goddamndest thing I've ever seen." Swiveller laughed. He made another trip to the truck and returned with a toilet brush and a bottle of bleach. Scrubbing the shit with the brush, he rinsed the walls and seats with water and wiped them dry.

"Like it never happened."

"You're crazy, Swiveller," Nubbins said. "You wouldn't catch me cleaning up after these bums."

"I'm aware of that. Still, it's no worse here than cleaning up after those pig idiot fucks over at Cypress Grove."

Cypress Grove Park was lush and beautiful but it was a pain in the ass to maintain. The patrons were generally successful, urbane and affluent. The drunks, the failures, the misshapen and the ugly all avoided the place. Yet it still took hours to pick up all the debris scattered throughout the park—plastic BPA-free water bottles, many still full of filtered water, empty bottles that once contained expensive craft beer or Beaujolais, soiled diapers, abandoned collapsible chairs and baby strollers, coats, hats, bathing suits, towels, and little green bags of dog shit. Dog walkers, if they bothered with it at all, simply scooped up their dogs' shit into the bags and left it there on the grass, often within sight of a waste bin. The trick in those cases was to take hold of the bottom of the bag with your long-handled trash grabber, shake out the contents, dispose of the plastic bag and leave the shit where you found it.

Nubbins would never admit it but the restrooms in Cypress Grove were often in a worse state than the porta-johns under the bridge. Kids enjoyed themselves by pissing and shitting on the floors, even smearing their excrement on the walls. They set the paper on fire and, on holidays like the 4th of July, blew up the toilets with M-80s.

"The Nub is right." Mayor Tuck winked at Swiveller. "You are a goddamn nut. You need to get it together. Be more like Nub. He ain't no bum. In fact, he's the hardest working taxpaying son of a bitch I know. He says so himself."

"Damn right," Nubbins nodded solemnly. His phone chirped. Nubbins read the text, chuckled and snapped the phone shut.

"Gwendolyn is finally on her way. She'll be here either this week or next." Nubbins beamed.

"Who is Gwendolyn?" inquired Madeleine.

"You're not going to believe this, Maddy, but Nub here has a girlfriend." Swiveller grinned. "By the way, Nub, you said yesterday her name was Alice."

"No I didn't."

"Yes, you did. And then you went on about how the name Alice was a sign because Alice was the name of your sister who died of cancer."

Nubbins paused for a moment then answered, "Oh yeah. Well, Alice is actually her middle name."

"With Nub, you never step in the same pile of bullshit twice," cracked Mayor Tuck.

"Shut up, Tuck. You don't believe me? Well, believe this, asshole."

Nubbins opened his billfold and carefully pulled out a photograph. He handled it gingerly, reverently, like it was an authentic scrap of the Dead Sea Scrolls. Mayor Tuck reached a hand for it. Nubbins batted it away.

"Hey, hands off."

They all craned their necks forward and studied the photograph. Swann and Fly Swatter even tottered over and joined in. The picture showed a shapely large-breasted young woman wearing sunglasses and a bikini standing on an ocean beach.

"What does a bimbo like that see in a fat old man with no teeth who lives in a dirty trailer full of junk with his bum of a son? Madeline laughed.

"It's called love, you drunken hag. Besides, I've already lost 40 pounds. I'm down to a 36-inch waist and even that's getting too big."

Nubbins reached back and tucked the tail of his gray parks department shirt into the waistband of his dirty jeans. He didn't bother with the front. Though his jeans were baggy in the ass and legs they were torque-wrench tight at the waist and worn low to accommodate his enormous overhanging belly and side pouches.

"You are looking pretty trim these days, Nubbins," said Madeleine with a wry smile.

"Damn right. I'll be in even better shape when she gets here. Not that she cares. She loves me as I am. She has definitely walked away with my heart."

"Walked away with your heart? You're going to make me sick with that shit."

Nubbins glared at Swiveller. "What the hell do you know about anything? You never have a woman. The only time you ever leave your house is when you go to work."

"Bullshit. I make it to where I need to go."

"Like where?"

"I don't know. Grocery store. Library. There was a time I couldn't even cross the street so I'm doing okay."

"You're a loner, Swiveller. You'll always be a loner."

"That's exactly what the palm reader told me at the state fair 35 years ago. Cost me a buck. I was 17 and stoned out of my brain. She told me I had to do something, perform some task within two or three years. If I didn't, I'd be isolated for the rest of my life."

"What were you supposed to do?" said Mayor Tuck.

"She didn't say. I don't think she knew. It sounded like a big deal, though, dramatic and exciting, like a quest for the Vase of Soissons or even the Holy Grail itself."

"Well, whatever it was, you fucked it up." Nubbins chortled.

"You're right. You know, Nubbins, you're a seer. When you quit the parks you ought to join the carnival."

"Fuck that. I'm not going to work at all. I'm going to take life easy."

"What about Arthur?" asked Madeleine. "I guess you'll have to give him the boot when Gwendolyn gets here."

"No, she loves Arthur."

Nubbins had two kids. One was in prison for murder. The other, Arthur, was in his thirties and lived with Nubbins in the trailer. Occasionally Arthur rode around with Nubbins

23

collecting junk out of dumpsters for resale. Most of the time, however, he sat on the couch smoking cigarettes, playing computer games or watching Bonanza reruns on television. In public, Arthur walked with a cane, wincing and grunting at every step. Every few months he had to appear before a judge and show cause as to why he shouldn't be held in contempt of court for not paying support for his children.

"That's if this chick actually shows up," Swiveller remarked. "She keeps delaying her arrival."

"She'll be here alright. She's just waiting for her inheritance check which should be arriving any day now. Once she's here I'm quitting this goddamn job. I don't have to put up with you or any of the rest of these bums anymore. Gwendolyn is going to take care of me the rest of my life."

Nubbins quit the job a few weeks later. It was a bit later than he had planned but circumstances had changed. Gwendolyn never did show up. As it turned out, Gwendolyn was actually a hacker named Arman living somewhere in Kazakhstan.

Nubbins seemed to be alright after receiving the news and managed to laugh it off, in public at least. But a week or so later he called in sick. The very next day a letter arrived, addressed to the head of the department, announcing Nubbins' immediate retirement. The letter, a long, rambling and incoherent account of the psychological and emotional abuse he endured at the hands of his coworkers and superiors, closed with the lines, "You can stick this job up your ass. No hard feelings."

Under the bridge, Swiveller emptied the overflowing cans and picked up and disposed of the scattered litter—rolled up disposable diapers, clothing, shoes, bibles, food rotting on paper plates, plastic water bottles, beer cans, crumpled religious tracts and what not. Boxes of used clothing, food and household supplies appeared on the sidewalk every day, usually dumped by religious groups. Very little of the swag was usable, however. It was mostly dusty old junk from people's closets—threadbare sport coats, high-heeled shoes, 70s era leisure suits, flip-flops, football cleats, catcher's mitts. The food, mostly boxes of macaroni and cheese and spaghetti, required cooking so was useless as well.

"There's a sick bat over there on the wall. You need to do something."

Madeleine sat at the table with Swann drinking 211. Her eye was black and swollen.

"What happened to you?"

"Crazy Tracy."

"Jesus. Everybody has a black eye today. What's going on around here?"

"I don't know. Weird vibes lately. But forget that. What are you going to do about the bat?"

"What's wrong with it?"

"It's sick. I think it's dying. It's just hanging on the wall."

"It's not dying, it's asleep. Just leave it alone."

"You'll see. I'll be right back."

Madeleine took a long hit of beer, got up from the table and headed off.

"Yeah, you'll see," Swann said. With both eyes blackened and puffy and his long, stringy red hair he looked like a red-headed Alice Cooper.

"Who did you tangle with, Swann?"

"Ray. The fucker ripped me off on some food stamps. I tried to kick his ass but forgot about that club he keeps behind the counter."

Ray, a paroled felon and notorious con artist, was the proprietor of Ray Mart, a nearby convenience store the drunks frequented. He swapped cash for food stamps, usually at 50 cents on the dollar. Sometimes he'd just pocket the stamps and tell the customer to go fuck himself. And since it was an illegal transaction to begin with, there wasn't much the customer could do about it aside from beating Ray's ass, or attempting to.

A short while later Madeleine returned with an old shoe box. She carefully pulled off the lid. Inside was a tiny bat.

"Goddamn it, Madeleine, I told you to leave that thing alone. It was fine where it was."

"No it wasn't. It was dying. I'll take care of it until it gets dark. Then I'll let it go."

"Now that you've fucked with it, it'll probably die for sure. You better let it go now, before it bites you. Ever hear of rabies? Put it somewhere out of the way and leave it alone."

"You know, Swiveller, a bat is a living creature just like you," Swann said sagely. "All life is sacred."

"Good grief. You sound like William Blake," observed Swiveller.

"Willy? Oh yeah, he's a good dude. We get drunk together once in a while."

Madeleine walked over to 16th street and plopped down on the curbing. She opened the box and cooed at the bat. Abruptly the tiny creature awoke and hopped out onto the busy road. With a long crooked stick Madeleine tried to retrieve it. Still groggy, it tried to fly away but could only flop about. A passing car crushed it into the asphalt.

Swiveller sighed and continued his work picking trash. He passed Roller's table. Roller was an intense looking character with tiny piercing eyes; he wore a black Satan goatee and an Alpine Fedora. He turned the crank on his machine, injecting tobacco into a paper tube. Pulling off the newly formed cigarette, he inspected it and put it the tray with the others near the sign that advertised Cheap Smokes, 10 Cents.

As Roller worked, some woman Swiveller had never seen before had his shirt pulled up and was squeezing the pimples on his back. She squinted intently though the curling smoke of the cigarette hanging from her lip.

"Ouch, goddamn you," winced Roller.

"Sorry," the woman said indifferently, wiping her fingers on her jeans.

Swiveller suddenly felt a sharp pain in his shoulder. He turned to find Mayor Tuck demonstrating the knowledge of pressure points he had learned in prison.

"If I move my hand farther up, it'll really hurt."

"Cut it out, Tuck. It hurts enough already. Where's your black eye?"

"What black eye?" Mayor Tuck eased his grip.

"Half the people here have black eyes; I figured you'd have one too."

The old man chuckled. "Well, the day isn't over yet. You know, the Nub was here yesterday."

"Really? This is the last place I'd ever expect to see him."

"Yeah, he borrowed 20 bucks. Said he's pulling 12,000 dollars a month from his gold mine up in Quartzburg but there's some temporary mix-up at the bank so he was short of cash."

"You think you'll ever see your 20 bucks?"

"Probably not. Those gold mines can be unpredictable. Have you heard from him?"

"Not a peep. I heard he's holed up in his trailer and won't answer the door. I suspect he's got quite a few bill collectors and skip tracers out looking for his ass."

"I think they found him. While he was here he pulled up his shirt and showed me the damage—massive bruises over his entire torso. He said he fell but it looks more like somebody went after him with a baseball bat."

"Fuck a duck," said Swiveller with a shudder.

"How much did he end up sending to that dude in Pakistan or wherever?" Mayor Tuck asked.

"3,500 bucks. He borrowed it from some loan shark in Garden City. 38 percent interest."

"Man, that poor dumb son of a bitch must have been really horny. There goes his pension."

"He's doesn't have a pension. He only worked for the department for three years."

"Doesn't matter, I suppose. Who needs a pension when you have a gold mine? Well, I'm off to Ray Mart. That Ray is a son of a bitch but he makes a hell of a cup of coffee."

Swiveller walked with Mayor Tuck to the edge of the dirty sidewalk where they stood and watched the cars speed by.

"Don't get hit. Madeleine almost bought it the other day."

"That's because Madeleine is an idiot. Crossing is easy. All you do is look down the street and see if any traffic is coming. If not, you can cross."

Mayor Tuck stepped from the shade of the bridge onto the hot asphalt. In the distance the pavement appeared to buckle and roll and eventually wash into an endless sea. He walked in that direction.

WHEEZER AND NEEDLE BOB SAT ACROSS from each other under the Chautauqua, drinking beer, waiting for the grub. About 20 people were huddled under the tent, smoking, scratching, fidgeting, and picking at themselves. It was a cold day and the wind was a killer.

Wheezer's broken and duct-taped radio squawked out old country music—"*She told me not to smoke it, but I did, and it took me far away. And I turned out to be, the only hell my momma ever raised…*"

"I don't know how you can listen to that whiney crud," said Needle Bob.

"That's Johnny Paycheck. He's the real deal. He tells it like it is," replied Wheezer, coughing and lighting a non-filtered Basic. Wheezer was a war vet. He had gotten the bottom half of his leg blown off in Vietnam. He had a defective prosthetic that functioned like a pirate's peg. The way Wheezer had it figured was they had this old pile of prosthetic legs in a warehouse at the V.A., and when some poor bastard needed a leg, they just grabbed one from the top of the pile.

"You don't look so good, Bobby," said Wheezer, pulling his jacket collar tighter around his neck.

Needle Bob scratched his face and head, as if to rid himself of some invisible insects. "I'm in serious need of some devil dust," he said, "but I'm flat broke. You heard I'm dying, right?"

"Yeah, you told me. Hepatitis."

"Hepatitis C, man," said Needle Bob. "It kills your liver." He took a long pull from his 24-ounce can of 211, cheap and powerful, 8.1 percent alcohol, marketed especially for down and out drunks on a budget. Wheezer liked to take things a little slower. He drank Milwaukee's Best. He didn't need as much as he used to. His own liver was half shot.

"You grew up in the wrong generation, Bobby," commented Wheezer with a wet-sounding cough. "Back in my day it was pot and peyote. Now it's either heroin or some nasty shit made from acetone and Drano.

Needle Bob belched. "Turn the radio off, Wheeze. That son of a bitch Pastor Billy is about ready to blow. I'm starved."

Once a week, The Billy Roper Ministries hosted a free lunch for the riffraff in the park. A former college football player, Pastor Billy was stocky with a muscular build. With his close cropped hair and large flattened nose he resembled a drill sergeant. Nobody could eat until Billy preached his sermon. Billy had only one sermon and Wheezer and Needle Bob had listened to it every week for months. Billy always described how he had one day seen Jesus in the flesh and Jesus had commanded him to go into real estate. Billy's obedience to the dictates of Jesus changed his life. He made a pile of dough and became a multimillionaire at 35. This qualified Billy for the ministry. According to Billy, salvation through Jesus and obedience to the Word were the keys to a life of success and wealth, on earth as in heaven. Disobedience and unbelief, on the other hand, landed you in a morass of poverty, destitution, alcoholism, and sloth. "And if you ain't careful," Billy always said, "God'll slap you into Hell so fast your feet won't even touch the ground."

Once the sermon was finally over, Wheezer and Needle Bob got up and stumbled over to the queue to receive their bologna sandwiches, potato chips, and milk from a couple of well-furred and heavily made-up women with the chiseled features of crows. "Just once," said Needle Bob, "I wish Jesus would appear to Pastor Billy and tell him to shut his fuckin' hole. Or at least write something different. That sermon's a killer." The servers apparently overheard Needle Bob. He only got half a sandwich. Wheezer and Needle Bob sat back down at the table and were chewing and smacking when Weatherby shuffled into the tent.

"What are you doing?" Needle Bob asked. "You never eat here. You hate people."

"I like *you* guys. Has the lawgiver laid it on yet?" he asked. "I'm half starved."

"Yeah, you missed it," said Wheezer.

"Good," said Weatherby, picking his nose with his pinky. "The keeper of the silver shekels has spoken." He made a loud lip fart. "And now we may eat." He set his pack down on the table with a thud. Sipping wine from his George's Cycles sports bottle, he headed off for the food line. Weatherby was the only wino that anyone knew who actually drank wine.

"You never know," said Needle Bob to Wheezer. "Billy might be right. We could be on the *highway to hell.*" He grimaced and hit a couple of power chords on his invisible guitar. His dirty blond hair hung in strings down to the middle of his back. Under his black trench coat he wore a threadbare Megadeth concert t-shirt. His skin-tight black pants were pegged at the ankles, his skinny legs resembling a couple of dried-up eels. He was constantly strung out and had lost his last job as a carny after The Rocket to the Moon, a carnival ride he was running, collapsed, injuring some little kids.

"Ah, you're as nuts as he is," said Wheezer. "You listen to too much of that doom and gloom metal shit."

"It tells it like it is," said Needle Bob solemnly. "The world is evil. People are always trying to fuck you. I was in two fights last week. It felt good to beat the shit out of some motherfuckers. It's a good thing I'm ripped." He pulled up a snot-streaked black sleeve to show off his atrophied muscles and collapsed veins. His skin was pocked, scabbed, bleached, and striated—like an old piece of driftwood.

Weatherby sat down at the table with his food and immediately had half a sandwich in his mouth. "I haven't seen you guys in months," he said, smacking loudly and breathing heavily through his nose. "Are you still at war with the V.A., Wheeze?"

"Sure am," said Wheezer. "It's become a pastime. I got escorted out by the MPs the other day. The bitch at the prescription counter said I was disorderly. All I said was I needed my fucking inhaler. I mean, I could barely get my breath, and she'd already made me wait for two hours while she sat and filed her goddamned nails. I couldn't take it any longer."

"Did you ever get your inhaler?" asked Weatherby.

"Yeah, but I had to beg the MPs and then apologize to Her Manicured Highness. To get by, you have to bow and scrape now and then."

"I can dig that," said Needle Bob. "Every time I see my probation officer I make a point to kiss his ass. Hey, did you hear Donna Jo's in prison?"

"The last I heard she was in county," said Weatherby.

"Not any more. Now she's doing seven years in the penitentiary for forging OxyContin prescriptions. Plus she had a bunch of priors. After Donna Jo went to the joint I started banging her sister, Deena. Now Deena's in jail."

"You sure know how to pick 'em," said Wheezer.

"So, I have bad luck with women. What about you and your nutty wife?"

"I'm divorcing her," said Wheezer. "I split after the domestic violence bust. I spent a month in jail for nothing. What would you guys do if some crazy chick came after you with a knife? You'd bust her in the chops is what you'd do. It was self defense, pure and simple. But she lied about the knife and I had to do the time."

"I never see you with a woman, Weatherby," said Needle Bob. "How come you're such a loner?" asked Needle Bob.

"Because I like peace and quiet," replied Weatherby. "Besides, I've lost all interest in fucking."

"Don't you get lonely?" asked Wheezer.

"Sure, I'm lonely all the time," said Weatherby. *'It's the loneliest feeling in the world to find yourself standing up when everybody else in sitting down. To have everybody look at you and say, "What's the matter with him?"'*

"What the hell was that?" said Needle Bob.

"*Inherit the wind*, my favorite play. I've read it at least a dozen times. I have most of it memorized."

"You memorized a play?" said Wheezer. "Jesus, I thought *I* led an exciting life."

"I take it you guys have never read *Inherit the Wind.*"

"No, I haven't," said Needle Bob irritably. "And I'm not interested in hearing any of it recited either."

"It might do you some good to read a book now and then, Bobby," said Wheezer. "All you do is listen to that metal shit."

"You're damn right," said Needle Bob. "The crunchier the better." He suddenly sat up rigidly erect, banging away at his invisible guitar and contorting his face into the simpering expression of a dissipated rock star. He looked as if he were straining to utter something profound, but instead slumped down and laid his head on the table, completely spent.

"You better get something down you, Bobby Boy," said Weatherby. "You look like you're about to have a goddamn seizure." He reached into his pack and produced a bottle of Old Grand-Dad. "Here drink this. I got it for my birthday but I can't stand the swill. I've been carrying it around for a week."

Needle Bob accepted the bottle and took a long pull. Tiny rivulets of whiskey dribbled from the corners of his mouth. "Thanks Weatherby," he said. "The way I feel, it won't be long before I'm partyin' with the devil."

Weatherby stood up and pulled his pack straps over his shoulders. "I'm heading up to Barker Gulch. You guys want to go?"

"What for?" asked Wheezer. "Barker Gulch is a good hoof from here."

"Wanda had her baby the day before yesterday," said Weatherby. "She's hiding out from Doug Gruel after that last beating he gave her. Gruel's in jail and will probably go to the joint but Wanda is still afraid that somehow he'll be released. I'm surprised she didn't lose the baby. Doris Brown helped her have it."

"Doris Brown?" snorted Needle Bob. "That's a laugh. It's a miracle the baby came out in one piece." His grinned and rubbed his bleary eyes. He seemed to be feeling better. He took another pull from the bottle.

"I hear you," said Weatherby. "Old Doris was as drunk as ever but she somehow managed to pull her head out of her ass. The baby's healthy."

"So where's Wanda camped?" asked Wheezer.

"She's up the gulch a ways, along Cottonwood Creek. She's got a nice hollowed-out place in the thickets. I told her I'd bring her a pack of smokes. Well, you want to go along or not?"

"Sure, why not?" said Wheezer. "How about you, Bobby?"

"Yeah, I'll go. But give me a minute," said Needle Bob. "I'm going to get more food."

"Good luck, said Wheezer. "Roper's not going to give you shit." Wheezer laughed himself into a hacking fit. He finally managed to cough up a wad of phlegm, which he spat on the grass floor.

"We'll see about that," said Needle Bob. He casually walked up to the food table and began to load his large coat pockets with sandwiches and milk. He was a good thief. No one noticed. Roper was preoccupied with praying over a couple of would-be converts. He had his hands on their heads like he was going to knock them together.

"Let's go," said Needle Bob, looking pleased with himself. The three tramps headed for Barker Gulch.

The icy wind blew the clouds rapidly across the dead-blue sky. Every now and again the sun shone red through what looked like a gaping wound, creating a kaleidoscope of sparkling color on the hard crusted snow. The tramps tried to avoid the busy areas of town. They kept to the labyrinthine alleys and narrow crooked streets. They passed through the old black section. Most of the houses were sagging and deserted. Crumbling walks ended abruptly where houses once stood. Overgrown fescue and thistles had taken over the vacant lots.

Once downtown, the tramps couldn't avoid the pushy holiday crowds. Shoppers crowded the icy sidewalks, carrying large multicolored bags. They gave the tramps a wide berth, as if they were hideous apparitions from the grave.

The cold wind whipped down streets flanked by department stores, banks and glitzy bars. Wheezer stumped along on his prosthesis, breathing hard, his breath whistling in and out of his lungs like a bird song. Needle Bob sweated profusely in the cold. His hands trembled as he held the collar of his trench coat above his ears. Every now and again he pulled out the bottle of Old Grand-Dad and took a hit. Weatherby drank wine from a sports bottle and recited, "...*Walking down an empty street, listening to the sound of your own footsteps. Shutters closed, blinds drawn, doors locked against you. And you aren't sure whether you're walking toward something, or if you're just walking away...*" Wheezer and Needle Bob said nothing.

At the edge of town, the snow-covered foothills loomed in the distance, the bluish whiteness of the slopes faintly luminescent. The snow-frosted trees creaked and groaned against the screeching wind, their bare branches grasping and clutching at the air, as if to grab onto immortality.

The three tramps came upon an old salvage yard surrounded by a chain link fence topped with razor wire. Signs along the length of the fence warned: "Attack Dog on Duty."

Inside was a jungle of discarded machinery, rusted-out hulks of automobiles, and piles of culverts, ducts, and iron pipe. Under the blanket of snow, the yard looked like an abandoned concentration camp scattered with hundreds of lime-coated corpses.

"I need to get in there," said Weatherby.

"What are you going to do, climb over that razor wire? And what about the goddamned attack dog?" said Wheezer, taking a puff of albuterol.

"There's no dog. That's bullshit. I know the way in. I sleep here sometimes." Weatherby walked down the length of fence, pulled back a clump of Sagebrush, and ducked through a hole cut in the chain link.

"What do you need in there for anyway?" asked Needle Bob, but Weatherby had already kicked open the door of an old shed and was inside. He re-emerged moments later with a roughly four-foot square scrap of corrugated sheet metal. He heaved it over the fence and was through the hole.

"What's that for?" said Wheezer.

"It's a roof for Wanda," replied Weatherby. "The thickets keep out most of the wind, but the snow can still get it. I'll probably get stuck by a few thorns but I can wedge it into the branches."

"Who's going to carry the damn thing?"

"I will," said Weatherby.

The tramps continued on. Once they passed the ruins of the old sanitarium that had housed shell-shocked WWI soldiers, the road ended at a narrow footpath. Snow-covered Sage and Bitterbrush lined the twisting trail. Weatherby had to walk sideways to negotiate the awkward sheet metal down the path. He sweated and cursed.

They entered a canopy of Cottonwoods where their way sloped down to Cottonwood Creek. The creek was dry. It only ran during the spring runoff. Wheezer had trouble with the slick rounded rocks of the dry creek bed. "I wish the damned V.A. would get me a leg with a foot that actually worked. This one's good for shit."

A hundred yards or so down the creek they came to an opening in the thickets.

"Knock knock," said Weatherby.

No response from inside.

"Wanda?"

"That you, Weatherby?"

"Yes, it's me. Plus a couple of Greeks bearing gifts."

"Shut up and get your ass in here."

The tramps entered a large canopied clearing. Over the years, numerous squatters had trod layers of leaves, bottle caps, broken glass, and cigarette butts into the hardened ground. Tiny shafts of gelid light shone through the branches, illuminating the debris and creating patterns of colorful mosaic. The thickets kept the wind out. The Sanctuary was still and quiet.

Wanda lay on a tattered patchwork quilt nestled in a kind of apse at the rear of the clearing. She was wrapped in a dirty, army-green wool blanket, her back propped up on an old sofa cushion. Her dark hair was tousled and streaked with dirt. The scar on her cheek and the deep furrows around her eyes suggested a life of endless battles and failed strategies. Weatherby gave Wanda the pack of cigarettes.

"Thanks, Weatherby," said Wanda. "I hope you guys didn't tell anybody else you were coming up here. I don't want Dougie to find out where I am. The son of a bitch tried to kill me. "

*"He that troubleth his own house shall inherit the wind,"* said Weatherby solemnly.

"Huh?" said Wanda, scrunching her face and looking quizzically at him.

"Don't mind Weatherby," said Wheezer, "he's been on that jag all day. Wanda, Doug's in jail and he's probably not getting out any time soon."

"I don't know. I don't think jail can hold that crazy son of a bitch. I'm scared that at any moment he's going to bust out, find me, and finish the job. I always seem to slip through the cracks."

Needle Bob sat down heavily on the hard ground. He took a substantial hit from his bottle. "Doug Gruel is a puss," he slurred. "If he comes after you, let me know and I'll beat his ass. I'm ripped." He pulled up his sleeve to show her his emaciated arm. Wanda didn't seem to be reassured.

"Where's the baby?" asked Wheezer. "Weatherby told us you had a baby."

Wanda reached her right arm over to her left side and gently pulled down the blanket, revealing a tiny, red, pinched face. The baby was sleeping, nestled between Wanda's breast and arm.

"What kind is it?" slurred Needle Bob.

"What do you mean what kind?" said Wanda. "She's a regular baby."

Needle Bob tried again. "Is it a boy or a girl?"

"She is a girl," Wanda said, passing her hand gently over the baby's forehead. "I named her Sparrow. She's going to fly out of here someday."

Needle Bob stared at the baby, then blinked his eyes, and said, "Are you hungry, Wanda? I've got some sandwiches and some milk."

"I'm starved," she said. "Where'd you get the food?"

"I swiped it from Billy Roper," said Needle Bob, his chest swelling like a rooster's. "His favorite Bible quote is 'He who does not work ought not to eat.' I'd say he's full of shit, wouldn't you?" He pulled the loot from his pockets and presented it all to Wanda.

"You're going to hell, Bobby," Wanda said with a smile.

"That's exactly what Roper says. But I still got some milk for the baby."

"She's already got milk," said Wanda.

"How's that?" asked Needle Bob, looking befuddled.

"My tits, you dumb ass. They're not just for men to paw

on," replied Wanda with a yawn. She turned to Weatherby. "What's with that chunk of metal you got there?"

"I thought I might wedge it up in the branches above you," Weatherby replied. "It'll help keep the snow off."

"It's not going to fall on me, is it?" Wanda said doubtfully.

"I'll make sure it doesn't," Weatherby answered.

He had to straddle Wanda and the baby to put up the sheet metal. He wedged it into the Russian olive branches, and as he feared, the long thorns stabbed and scratched his bare hands. They were bleeding and red from the cold by the time he finished. "It's up there pretty good," he said. "It ain't' going nowhere."

"You're pretty handy, Weatherby, for a guy who talks shit all the time," said Wanda.

"Don't encourage him, Wanda," said Wheezer. "He'll start in again on that play or some goddamn poem and we'll never get him to shut up." He handed Wanda his duct-taped radio. "You better take this. It must get pretty lonely up here."

"You're giving me your radio?" said Wanda. "You've had that thing forever."

"Yeah, I'm getting tired of it. I need to get a new one. Well, we better get going. It'll be dark soon."

"See you, Wanda," said Needle Bob, rising unsteadily and offering her the remainder of the whiskey. "You want the rest of this?"

"Sure," she said. She tipped the bottle and killed it.

Weatherby smiled at Wanda and the sleeping baby. "We'll be back to check on you," he said. "Things are going to be alright."

"Thanks, you guys," Wanda said with a wave.

Wheezer, Needle Bob, and Weatherby headed back down Cottonwood Creek. Wanda had turned on the radio. The tramps could hear the King of Rock and Roll as they stumbled down the creek bed:

*"Got no sleigh with reindeer, no sack on my back,*
*You're gonna see me comin' in a big black Cadillac.*
*Whoa, it's Christmas time, pretty baby,*
*And the snow is fallin' on the ground.*
*Well you've been a real good little baby;*
*Santa Claus is back in town."*

The sun was beginning to set. The limbs of the Cotton-woods moved stiffly like ancient, gnarled fingers, black against the brilliant orange of the clouds. By the time they reached the footpath, the King had faded away into the wind.

**W**HAT MADE THE MEMORIAL RIDICULOUS
was the tramps didn't even like One-Beer Bob.
Yet when they learned he was dead, found
drowned and decomposed in the creek, the
tramps immediately set to work building him
a monument, a huge cone-shaped heap of river
rocks. It sat in the center of the clearing between the picnic tables and the old fireplace. On
top, a warped and splintered square of plywood
served as a plaque, adorned with a cartoonish
flower. Around the flower were scrawled various inscriptions of sentimental doggerel and
cryptic nonsense.

Dick Swiveller set his rake and bucket down
in the litter of beer cans and cigarette butts at
the base of the mound. He read the inscriptions.
One in particular caught his eye:

*When there was no blood*
*There was only water*

Swiveller read it aloud and laughed.

"What a lot of horseshit."

"Let me tell you something, college boy,"
said Sister Christian. "When you're really up
against it, you'll take whatever comfort comes
your way, even if it is horseshit." She was seated
at her usual place under the Sycamore tree with
Don McGough and Captain Kirk. Though it
wasn't even 9 a.m., the table top and surrounding ground were littered with empty beer cans,
crunched and scattered.

BURN

"Alright, I hear you," said Swiveller. "It's odd, though. You guys didn't even like One-Beer Bob. Yet you went to all this work to pile up a bunch of rocks for him."

"That's what you do when someone dies. You make a pile of rocks. Haven't you ever heard of the pyramids?" Sister Christian was annoyed at having to school Swiveller in the obvious. "Bob was a brother. We had our differences, but he was a brother."

"Damn right," said Captain Kirk, scratching the bald spot at the top of his military buzz cut. Captain Kirk's story was he spent 17 years in the army as an airborne ranger. He always wore the same set of dirty camouflaged fatigues and combat boots. Lately he had taken to camouflaging his face. Every morning he painted on whatever was at hand—mud, tar, rust, the juice from grass clippings and so on.

"Well, in any case," said Swiveller, "the saying has it backwards. I mean, there's always been plenty of blood, fucking rivers of the shit, since the beginning of time. It's water that's always been scarce."

He looked up at the leaden gray smoke hanging heavy in the sky. It hadn't rained a drop since spring and the wildfires had been burning unabated for more than six weeks. The acrid smoke blocked out the sun, leaving the earth in dull hazy shadows.

"By the way, Sis, that's a pretty good flower you drew," Swiveller said, pulling a rag from his pocket and wiping the dirty sweat from his face. "I didn't know you could draw."

"I took drawing in high school," Sister Christian replied, tipping back a can of beer and softly belching. "I used to do a lot of things." Some of the beer dribbled onto her faded denim jacket. She scooped up the foaming liquid with her fingers and licked them. She'd worn the exact same style of jacket for years, along with faded, skin-tight denim jeans and granny boots. Every now and then she rooted through the free bins at the front of thrift stores looking for her style. Occasionally she hit pay dirt and got a change of clothes.

Swiveller bent down and pulled a dirty pink teddy bear from his bucket and handed it to Sister Christian. "I believe this is yours," he said.

Sister Christian snatched the bear. "Nikki Sixx! I've been looking for him everywhere. I thought he had left me for good."

She kissed the pink stuffed animal on the face and adjusted the soiled white ribbon around its neck. Clutching the bear, she rose unsteadily from the table. With her free arm she hooked Swiveller around the neck and drew him close. "Thank you," she slurred in his ear. Her breath was hot and smelly, like a fart through an electric heater. "Where on earth did you find him? I was so worried."

"He was buried under a pile of junk up at that god-damned fort," replied Swiveller, gently disengaging himself from Sister Christian and helping her to her seat.

"It was a fuckin' good fort. And you just went and tore hell out of it," said Don McGough with a scowl. He hawked up a wad of phlegm and spat. "We go to all that work and you go fuck it all up. What an asshole." He combed his long blond hair back behind his big protruding ears with his fingers and replaced his backwards ball cap. McGough spent a lot of time preening. "Chicks don't like sloppy motherfuckers," he always said. Though there was no sun, he put on his sunglasses, taking care not to poke his swollen black eye or the bluish yellow contusions on his cheeks.

"I told you guys that fort had to come down," said Swiveller. "More than once."

"My ass. You didn't say shit about it. Not to me, anyhow."

"Don't play dumb, Don," said Swiveller. "We talked about it last week."

"Look, Swiveller, I don't want to hear anymore of

your lies," said McGough. "I just want to know what you did with all my property. Where are my goddamn clothes? Where is all my weaponry?"

"Just like I told you, I put everything I found in the dumpster. It was all junk anyway, filthy and disgusting."

"More lies," said McGough. "That fort and everything in it was clean and new. We ain't pigs." He flicked a fly from the tattoo on his forearm. The tattoo was an extremely sloppy representation of a naked woman wrapping herself around a dagger. The tattoo extended from wrist to elbow. McGough was proud of it, especially of the fact that he himself was the artist. The project helped pass the time during McGough's long bit in state prison.

"Because of you we're all fucked," said McGough. "Just look at that sky. It's a sign, man. The shit'll be coming down any day. But now we got no place to ride out the earthquakes and the tsunamis. We got no fort and no weapons to fight off the starving mobs. Fuck you, Swiveller."

"What can I say, Don? It's a public park. You can't fight the Battle of Armageddon in a public park. You can probably still retrieve your stuff, though. The dumpster hasn't been emptied yet this week."

"I ain't rootin' through no dumpster. You owe me some new clothes, motherfucker."

"Send me a bill, McGough." Swiveller wasn't in the mood to argue. It had taken hours to haul the heavy stones and the railroad ties down the hillside, load it all up in the truck and take it back to the bone yard. And that didn't include the cleanup of all the trash, filthy bedding, soiled underwear and Don's stash of homemade weaponry—old dirty socks with the toes filled with rocks and nails, sharpened pieces of metal attached to wooden handles and 2-foot lengths of inch-thick rebar. Sometime in the future Swiveller would have to take a shovel and fill the deep notches McGough and Captain Kirk had dug into the hillside, the steps that led up to the fort.

"I need a favor, Swiveller," said Captain Kirk.

"Yes, what is it?"

"I need to borrow ten dollars so I can go the store and get a sandwich and some chocolate milk. I get paid on the 15th and I'll pay you back then."

The 15th of each month was always Captain Kirk's red letter day. Though he never had a job, he was always getting paid on the 15th. Or his sister was selling his house back home in Fairdealing, Missouri, and he'd have the money on the 15th. Or on the 15th he was finally going to walk the 500-odd miles to the coast of Oregon to see the Pacific Ocean, the final leg of his "walk across America." Captain Kirk had been on his famous walk for three years at least, though he had spent nearly all that time at the picnic table under the Sycamore.

"I just gave you ten yesterday," said Swiveller. "I can't give you money every day. Why don't you just fly a sign like everybody else?"

"Because I'm not a bum," said Captain Kirk, belching. I'm an airborne ranger."

"Well, you're going to nickel and dime me to death one of these days," said Swiveller.

"That's right, Captain," said Sister Christian. "You're a mooch. You bum off everybody."

"Get out of here. I've never bummed a dime in my life. I only borrow if I have to and I always pay my motherflippin' debts. I'm going to settle up with you on the 15th, Swiveller, come hell or high water."

"Okay, Captain," said Swiveller. "It's a deal."

McGough pulled a large tangle of rope from a black plastic sack and set it on the table. He and Captain Kirk set to work separating the varying lengths and colors and tying them together.

"What's all that about?" asked Swiveller.

"We're going to hang the motherflipper that killed our brother," said Captain Kirk.

45

"That's right," said McGough. "We're going to be having us a little necktie party before long. You're not invited, Swiveller."

"I appreciate that. Who are you going to hang?"

"Don't know yet," McGough replied. "We have to find the bastard first."

"Well, you knuckleheads will be lynching an innocent man. One-Beer Bob wasn't murdered. He was just wandering around drunk in the dark and fell in the creek. End of story."

Captain Kirk snorted. "How come his neck got broke then? Tell me that. Nobody gets a broken neck from falling into a creek. Maybe a lump on his fool head but not a broken neck."

"Yeah, and he'd just gotten his inheritance," said McGough. "The day before he died Bob was telling everybody and their dog that he had 1,500 dollars on him."

"And you believed that?" Swiveller laughed. "I suppose you also believed his bullshit about drinking only one beer a day."

Sister Christian broke out into a loud sustained laugh, which brought on a horrible sounding coughing fit. She finally managed to spit a large brownish blob onto the dirt.

"More blood," she said, smacking her lips with a sour expression. "This smoky air is killing me." She pulled a tube of lip gloss from her pocket and applied it in several circular strokes. Her lips were always shiny, unlike her face, which had the texture of a Brazil nut.

"You guys are listening to too much hooey," said Swiveller. "Bob's neck wasn't broken. That was just a rumor. I got the straight dope from Thorny."

"Officer Thornbeck? He's just blowin' it out his ass," said McGough.

"Don's right. Thorny is full of shit," said Captain Kirk. "Bob's neck was broke all right. Snapped clean in two. I should know. I'm the one that found him. I'm an airborne ranger. I know about broken necks."

Swiveller laughed. Captain Kirk had been chattering away to anyone and everyone his story of finding the corpse, a highly dramatic account illustrated by horrific and grotesque facial contortions. The truth was much more mundane. The bloated corpse of One-Beer Bob had been found by an elderly citizen out walking her dog. According to the coroner, the body had been there at least two weeks, with nobody the wiser including Swiveller, who regularly walked the bank picking up the discarded clothing and beer cans.

"Well," said Swiveller, rake in hand, "while you guys are forming your posse, I need to clean this place up."

"What for?" said Captain Kirk. "I picked up this morning, like I do every morning."

"Yeah," chimed in McGough. "We keep this place clean."

"I can see that," said Swiveller, surveying the scattered debris. "I appreciate the help."

He started with the picnic table. Cleaning under the table was a pain in the ass and Swiveller liked to get that part out of the way first. The worst of it was getting the tramps to move, which always involved considerable ass-dragging and complaining. "It'll only take a minute and then I'll have it back," he would say. The responses were the always same. "It's already clean here." "We picked up this morning." "This is bullshit." It took a delicate balance of negotiation and threats, but eventually the tramps got up and Swiveller dragged the 200-pound table from under the tree.

Once that part was finished and the table was back where it belonged, the tramps sat down again, adjusted their clothing and opened fresh beers. Swiveller began raking up the hundreds of cigarette butts and beer tabs, torn up citations, bits of shoestring, beer cans, soiled underwear, used rubbers, and so on.

"Hey Swiveller," said Captain Kirk.

"What now?"

"You got any lime?"

"Lime? What for?"

"Well, some of the brothers have been shitting behind the fireplace. It's getting pretty ripe back there."

Swiveller walked around to the back of the fireplace. Next to the stone wall sat an enormous stinking pile of shit crawling with legions of flies.

"Magnificent," said Swiveller. "Now that's an honest monument. I think you guys are on to something. It's a miniature pyramid. It says, 'Hey motherfucker, we were here.'"

"You've lost your mind, Swiveller," said Sister Christian, scowling.

"I know it," said Swiveller, walking back around, shaking his head. "What is wrong with you guys? The city provides you with a toilet. It's right fucking over there."

He pointed toward the orange portable toilet sitting idle in the parking lot. It was shrouded in haze but still visible.

"Hey man, that wasn't us," said Captain Kirk. "It was all those other drunken assholes. One-Beer Bob was one of them."

"That's right," said McGough. "I saw Bob shit there many times. All that runny beer stuff is his."

"Well, I guess One-Beer Bob needs to bury it."

"What is that supposed to mean?" said Captain Kirk. "Bob is dead."

"I mean I'm not cleaning that. It's ridiculous."

"You're talking crazy," said McGough. "You're the parkie. You've got to clean that shit up. It stinks."

"Yes, it does," replied Swiveller. He resumed his raking.

Swiveller had managed to finish about half the clearing when Trash Bag wandered over, got down on his hands and knees, and began combing through the litter. With his stumpy round body and his filthy clothes, he looked like an enormous hedgehog. Trash Bag never had any money for cigarettes so he scrounged the grounds and trash cans for snipes, twisting out the remaining tobacco into a little pouch. When he needed a smoke, he simply rolled up the recycled tobacco in a Zig-Zag paper—maybe newspaper if he was really hard up.

"I think those butts are all sniped out, Trash Bag" said Swiveller. "Why don't you just bum a regular cigarette?"

"I never have any luck bumming smokes," Trash Bag replied, his blackened face wet with sweat and his wild eyes moving around in all directions.

"Hey, somebody toss Trash Bag a cigarette," Swiveller said to the tramps. Captain Kirk and McGough predictably replied that they couldn't spare one. Sister Christian frowned at them, pulled a Marlboro from her handbag and tossed it to Trash Bag.

"Thanks, Sis," said Trash Bag. He plopped his ass down in the dirt cross-legged, weirdly eyeballing the factory-made cigarette from all angles as if it had just fallen from outer space. He fished around in his shirt pocket and produced a rolling paper. To everyone's amazement, he emptied the tobacco from Sister Christian's cigarette onto the paper, twisted it with his stubby fingers, licked it and lit up.

"It's been a while since I had a decent smoke," said Trash Bag, popping out smoke rings with his hairy jaw.

Captain Kirk and McGough burst out laughing. Sister Christian shook her head slowly from side to side and tossed Trash Bag another one. "You might as well take another for the road," she said.

Trash Bag scooped up the smoke, flashed Sister Christian a grin of mossy brown teeth, and headed off.

"Swiveller, I need a favor," said Captain Kirk.

"Now what? Christ, I've never get this done."

"I need a ride to the store to get some beer."

"In the city truck? You're high."

"Come on, give me a ride. I need a cigar, too."

"Forget it, Captain. I need this job."

"Ah, you're paranoid. You won't get caught. I'll duck down. Nobody will see me."

"You're drunk," said Swiveller. "Maybe you should go lie down or something. There's no fucking way I'm giving you a ride in the city truck."

Swiveller turned away from Captain Kirk and noticed McGough standing unsteadily on top of the picnic table clutching the completed rope and noose. "Goddamn this fuckin' park picnic table," McGough said. "It feels like it's on fuckin' rockers."

"Get off there," said Sister Christian, visibly annoyed.

"Keep your panties on," said McGough. He was trying to toss the noose over a sturdy mottled-green branch a few feet above his head. On the first attempt the noose flew wide. He tried again and this time it didn't even leave his hand.

"Fuckin' piece of shit rope," he said, sweat running down his bruised face. "A guy can't even get a decent rope anymore."

He heaved the rope up again with everything he had. The exertion caused him to step back, his dirty boot landing square on Sister Christian's pink bear, Nikki Sixx.

"You idiot fuck," growled Sister Christian, landing a solid punch on Don's calf. The punch caused his knee to buckle and he fell onto his ass on the edge of the table.

"Ouch, goddamn it. What the fuck, Sis?" said McGough, rubbing his calf. "You ridin' the cotton pony again?"

"You're starting to piss me off, Donnie. Get your ass off the table and throw that stupid rope in the trash can. Enough's enough." Sister Christian brushed off Nikki Sixx, inspected the pink bear closely and put him back on the table. "And if you ever say anything about me being on the rag again, I'm going to black your other eye."

Don rubbed his swollen cheeks, mementos of the last time he tangled with Sister Christian.

Swiveller finally began to make progress. Captain Kirk

and McGough sat silent and glum, their heads nodding slowly forward in the thick leaden air. They were nearly out. Sister Christian repetitively flicked an empty 211 can with her middle finger, watching Swiveller as if in a trance. The pinging sound was soothing, like a metronome.

"Are you going to leave the monument?" she said finally, tugging a strand of dried weed from her enormous lion's mane of hair.

"Sure. I'll leave it for a few days. If I leave it longer it'll get knocked down and scattered." Swiveller worked at bagging the large pile of debris he'd raked. His leather gloves were black with dirt and ashes.

"That's good. I hated One-Beer Bob but I'll still miss him. You know, I wish I had your job. I love that kind of work."

"You don't say."

There was another long pause. *Ping. Ping. Ping.* Sister Christian stared off into space, as if she were studying a tiny speck at the far edge of the universe.

"Yes," she said, "I love gardening."

Finished, Swiveller picked up the bags of debris and his tools and headed for the truck. He tossed the bags, the rake and the bucket in the bed, started the rig and headed for the exit. Just inside the park entrance from Americana Boulevard, Swiveller spotted Trash Bag lying on the sidewalk near the bus stop. Trash Bag often slept there, apparently soothed by the noise of the automobile traffic. Normally, Swiveller would have let him be but a small crowd of citizens had gathered. They wore white particle masks. Once was talking excitedly on a cell phone. In the hazy gloom, the scene reminded Swiveller of a Chernobyl documentary.

Swiveller got out of the truck and elbowed his way to Trash Bag. Trash Bag was lying flat on his back with his eyes closed, the cigarette Sister Christian had given him "for the road" dangling from his lips unlit. Swiveller lightly kicked the bottom of his shoe. "You all right, Trash Bag?"

"Yes," said Trash Bag, opening his eyes, pulling away the cigarette and smacking his lips. He raised his head slightly from the concrete.

"Thank you," he said.

Swiveller got in the truck and drove until it all disappeared.

A THICK FOG CHOKED CASTLE ROCK PARK—cold, suffocating, still. It was quiet, too quiet for Weatherby. His brain compensated for the lack of sound by providing a maddening, grinding hum, like the bowing of the lower registers of a cello. Weatherby slapped both ears but the hum remained.

Ernie began to growl and Weatherby heard the approaching footsteps. A shadowy figure materialized from the gloom, the parkie, Dick Swiveller. Swiveller approached the Spruce tree. Weatherby was seated in a rusted-out lawn chair near his tree, just in front of the doorway that led to his living quarters inside the boughs.

"Hey, Dick," he said as Ernie began to bark.

"Hey yourself," said Swiveller. "Don't let that dog take my leg off."

"Cut it out, Ernie," scolded Weatherby.

The tiny dog barked again at the approaching Swiveller, glanced at Weatherby, and trotted over to a wicker basket next to Weatherby's chair. Once in the basket, the dog completely covered itself with a tiny knitted blanket. Weatherby had knitted the blanket for Ernie. The project had taken him a couple of weeks, it being his first stab at knitting. The stitches were haphazard and uneven but it was wool and kept Ernie warm. Weatherby reached down and gently poked the little form under the blanket. The dog growled. Weatherby grinned mischievously at Swiveller. Ernie crawled from under the blanket and out of the basket. He reared on his hind legs, stretched out his forepaws to Weatherby's knee, and let out another bark. Weatherby scooped up the dog and placed him on his lap. Ernie continued to eye Swiveller, blinking and licking a forepaw. Weatherby had found Ernie abandoned one day in the park. Nobody came looking for the dog so Weatherby took him in.

"Looks like Ernie's taking life easy," said Swiveller

"Ernie's a bum," said Weatherby. The dog's eyes were half shut as Weatherby stroked the tiny head.

"Grab a chair, Dick. There's one just inside the doorway, there."

Swiveller wedged himself into a hole in the spruce boughs and pulled a chair from the darkness inside. He unfolded the rickety chair and sat down across from Weatherby and Ernie.

"So what's for breakfast?" said Swiveller.

"Nothing hot, I can tell you that," said Weatherby. "Some assholes crapped on my grill last night. Unbelievable. Two goddamn monster turds right on my grill. They're frozen now, stuck on like barnacles. I don't know if I'll ever get them off. But the worst of it is the idiots didn't even wipe their asses after they shit. There's no used paper around. How can a guy take a shit without wiping his ass? That's not right."

"When you gotta go, you gotta go," ventured Swiveller, laughing.

"Yeah, it's funny for you," said Weatherby with some annoyance. "You don't have to cook on that grill. Besides, every civilized human being knows to be prepared with paper when nature calls. It's common sense." Weatherby pulled up the stopper on his Adidas sports bottle and took a long pull of wine.

"You know," commented Swiveller, "When I see you drink out of that bottle, I'm almost fooled into thinking you're one of those dopey personal fitness trainers, or maybe a real estate broker, out for a morning jog and stopping for a hit of Gatorade. The only thing that gives you away is that shaggy beard."

"That's pretty funny, Dick. I can't believe you would associate me with scum like that." Weatherby said. "But seriously, idiots who drink from wine bottles in paper sacks are so goddamned obvious, they deserve to get popped. You have to be smart. You have to keep yourself under the radar."

Weatherby knew how to exist without leaving too many footprints. He bought cheap Franzia wine in the box, removed the plastic wine-filled pouch and hid it in his pack. He drank the wine from plastic containers he found in trash bins—worn sports flasks with scuffed logos and energy drink bottles with flavors like Fruit Punch and Cherry Pomegranate Splash. Anything red. Whenever he drained the bottle, it was a simple matter to fill it again from the hidden pouch. He used the empty cardboard box to kindle his fires.

"That's why you've managed to live in this park for, let's see, seven years now," said Swiveller, grimacing as he slowly rotated his shoulders. "And without any trouble to speak of."

"What's the matter with you?" asked Weatherby. "Stiff neck?"

"Just ordinary aches and pains. Seems like after 50 if it's not one thing it's another."

"Goes with the territory," said Weatherby sagely.

"Yeah. I feel like my old grand dad. He used to grunt and groan when he moved around. I remember when I was a kid I'd imitate him and make a joke out of it. Some joke. I'd really like to have that one back."

"Kids are fucking evil bastards," said Weatherby, pulling at his beard. The dog stood up on Weatherby's lap and began to pant. Weatherby set Ernie on the ground. The dog wandered around sniffing.

"A few weeks ago, I was reading about Martin Luther, you know, the Reformation dude, and I remember reading that he was taking a shit when he got his big famous illumination. Anyway, it was Luther's disgust with his own shit that led to his vision of the world as an evil place dominated by the devil. The world is shit. It stinks, it's black, and it's foul. Go over and take a big whiff of those two big sons of bitches lying on that grill; see for yourself."

"I know what shit smells like, Weatherby. I deal with it every day. But what in hell does that have to do with anything?"

"It has to do with those little bastards who crapped on my grill," said Weatherby. "They're really demons disguised as little bastards."

Swiveller sat for a moment and watched Weatherby puffing out smoke rings.

"Maybe you're right," said Swiveller. "That is, if it was kids who did it. Where do you come up with all these crazy ideas, anyway?"

"From the library, man," said Weatherby. "I find out about all kinds of stuff there. That's where I got the skinny on the CIA's involvement in the Kennedy assassination. And a lot of other stuff too. Sometimes I take Ernie in there to get warm."

"I thought you couldn't have dogs in the library," said Swiveller.

"Ernie is so small; I keep him in my coat. Nobody has ever noticed."

"So do you think all that is true about Luther?" said Swiveller.

"It's what the book said. But even if it isn't true," said Weatherby with a grin, "it ought to be."

"Spoken like a true theologian."

"How are things with the Parks Department?" Weatherby asked. "I see they kept you, even though you had to go to the cracker factory."

"The job's okay," responded Swiveller. "I'm on thin ice but

that's not unusual. I spent quite a bit of time yesterday at Arcadia cleaning up Fern and Roy's crap along Spring Creek."

Weatherby laughed. "Those two are the main attraction over there. More entertaining than the zoo and it doesn't cost you a nickel."

"They're fucking unbelievable," said Swiveller. "Garbage scattered everywhere—beer cans, shit-stained panties, cigarette butts, used bloody Kotex pads, old filthy clothes, adult diapers rolled up and loaded with gravy—you name it. I tell them all the time, this isn't your fucking house. You two don't live here. Not that it does any good. Yesterday Swanson and I filled nearly a dozen large trash bags with all kinds of crap—pots, pans, clothes, shoes, food, all rotten, filthy, crawling with vermin."

"I don't know how anybody can live in such filth," said Weatherby with disgust.

"Me neither. If it weren't for the constant mess, I wouldn't have an issue with those two. I used to tell them that. Be cool and keep your shit picked up, I'd say, and you won't have any grief from me. Not to mention the cops. But I gave up on the lectures long ago. Fern and Roy live the only way they know. Like us all, I guess. The problem is Arcadia is a goddamn public park and I work for the parks department. I don't bother with niceties anymore. I just show up and start shoveling. Whether they're there or not."

"I imagine that crazy Fern has something to say about that."

Swiveller laughed. "Oh yes. She says she's going to kill me and burn my house down."

"When is this going to happen?"

"Never. She's been saying that for years," Swiveller said with a sigh. "It's an ongoing battle. One that will outlast us all, I'm afraid."

"You're a bastard, Swiveller," said Weatherby, his grin revealing a set of blackened teeth. "You're always fucking up somebody's pad."

"I know it," Swiveller said, eyes glazed, as if in a trance. He had his pocket knife out and was whittling away at a thumbnail. "But the sun shines on the wicked too. Maybe it's the mood elevators and the tranquilizers but today I woke up from a weird dream I'll be damned if I can remember and I actually felt good, like today was going to be a good day. I suppose I really am going crazy."

"A good day?" said Weatherby, "With all this cold and fog? What kind of nonsense is that?"

"I don't know. I like the cold. By the way, thanks for coming to visit me at the hospital. I'm sorry they wouldn't let you in."

"They probably have a policy of no winos allowed," said Weatherby, filling his Adidas bottle.

"Actually, it's considered a privilege to have visitors other than family. I didn't get any privileges. They've got a level system gig in there. If you cooperate, you move up the levels. I wasn't in the mood to cooperate. The groups were boring and stupid and the nurses were bitches. So I stayed the entire week in the closed unit on Level 0. No visitors. No privileges."

"Jesus, what did you do the whole time?"

"I sat out in the lounge in front of the nurses' desk and read *Les Misérables*, the whole 1200 pages, man. Even the boring chapters that have nothing to do with the story. Reading about Jean Valjean freed me in a way. A couple of the orderlies were friendly and we bullshitted a little now and then. Once this crazy bastard in the room next to mine tried to club an orderly with this piece of metal he'd somehow torn off the door. The orderly kicked his ass. That was the high point of the week. Finally, the psychologist told me I was, as he put it, 'sabotaging my own treatment' and discharged me."

Swiveller stood up. "Well, I guess I better get started on that grill. I might have to chisel that crap off."

"I'll go over with you—hey, where's Ernie?" said Weatherby, looking around. "Do you see him, Dick?"

"Maybe he's under that blanket in the basket," said Swiveller.

Weatherby poked at the blanket. No response. He pulled off the little blanket, revealing the dog. Ernie opened his eyes, stood shakily, and barked.

"Ah, possuming, I thought so," said Weatherby. Ernie wagged his tail and barked again. "Come on, Dick, you'll get a kick out of this."

Swiveller and Weatherby headed off through the fog. Weatherby had his Adidas bottle in hand, and sipped from it from time to time. Ernie skittered alongside. Bare apple trees suddenly appeared from out of the mist, the skeletal branches reaching up into the fog. Castle Rock Park was built on the grounds of the old prison apple orchard. The grim sandstone walls of the abandoned prison still stood at the northernmost edge of the park. Just past the trees they arrived at the concrete pad upon which Weatherby's grill and some small tables were anchored.

"Now isn't that some repulsive motherfucking shit?" said Weatherby, indignant. "And look around you—no paper! You can bet your boots that *Luther* used paper."

"Far out, man," said Swiveller. "It's like modern art."

Two long gnarled turds lay frozen side by side on the grill, looking like some sort of ancient rune.

Swiveller looked around. "Fortunately that's all they did. Nothing's broken. There's no graffiti. It's probably a good thing Ernie didn't hear whoever it was and start barking. They'd have found your place. Hell, they might even have come over and squatted over you. Or set you on fire. That's been known to happen, you know."

"Yeah, no kidding," said Weatherby. "I guess I was pretty lucky. You think those damn things are going to come off?"

"Sure," said Swiveller. "It just might take a while. I'll need to get a few things from the truck."

Swiveller disappeared into the fog and reemerged a few

minutes later with a square-point shovel and a wire brush. Weatherby had his sports bottle in his dirty paw and was singing in a cracked, wheezing voice:

> *"If I weave around at night*
> *Policemen think I'm very tight*
> *They never find my bottle though they ask.*
>
> *"'Cause Plastic Jesus shelters me*
> *For his head comes off you see.*
> *He's hollow and I use him like a flask."*

"What? Are you singing hymns now?" asked Swiveller, setting to work on the grill. Ernie squatted under the table, gnawing away at a dog biscuit made to resemble a T-bone steak. He looked up from the steak occasionally and growled as if somebody was going to take it away from him.

Weatherby took a long drag of wine. "Hymns? What are you talking about? That's Billy Idol."

"Billy Idol?" said Swiveller. "I didn't know you liked Billy Idol. You're always telling me you hate rock music."

"I know," said Weatherby. "But a guy I know made me a CD with all kinds of stuff on it. I like that song."

"Well, the turds are coming right off. They must have frozen just as they hit the metal. A couple of minutes with a wire brush and it'll be like it never happened."

"I'll be goddamned," said Weatherby, watching Swiveller shovel the shit into a black plastic bag and brush the grill. "You're an amazement to me, Dick."

"Nothing to it," said Swiveller.

"I don't suppose a skill like that pays too well, though," said Weatherby.

"No."

"Probably doesn't get you much action with the women either."

"No," said Swiveller, picking up his tools and the plastic bag. "But it's all I've got."

It wasn't long after Swiveller left that the sun came out and burned away the fog. Birds chirped in the bare branches of the trees. A brown squirrel rooted about on the frozen ground. Weatherby got a fire going in the grill and cooked up a rasher of bacon. He then used the grease to fry up some sliced potatoes. He got his old percolator out and made some strong coffee. With Ernie asleep in his lap, he ate and sipped his coffee. It all seemed so easy.

THE OLD FIREPLACE WAS CRUMBLING AND blackened with age. The surrounding turf had long since been trodden into hardpan. The area was scattered with beer cans, soiled clothing, splintered scraps of wood, broken glass and countless cigarette butts. From the chimney rose thin wisps of acrid gray smoke.

Fat Jack stoked the fire and lumbered slowly the few steps back to the picnic table. The table sat in the shade of a black locust tree. Fat Jack was pushing sixty. He was narrow-shouldered yet enormously fat around the middle. He sat down heavily across from Toby Honeycutt, wincing as he rubbed the swelling on the side of his jaw from an abscessed tooth. Though it was early spring and the weather was still rather chilly, Fat Jack perspired heavily.

"Make sure that fire's good and hot," Toby said, picking absently at the clumps of dried skin on his pasty freckled forehead. "I'll gut the critter and get the meat ready as soon as I finish this beer." He took a long swallow from a silver 24-ounce can, picked up the carving knife, and ran his grimy thumb across the blade. Toby was shriveled and emaciated and clad in his usual dirty bib overalls and huge black janitor shoes.

Fat Jack nodded, wiped his wet forehead with his shirtsleeve and resumed work tearing the handles and chains off the battered trash can lids. The grill had long since been stolen from the fireplace, so meat was grilled on the undersides of trash can lids. The city parkies usually raised the devil about the boys tearing off the can lids, sometimes they even called in the cops, but what the hell, figured Fat Jack, a guy's gotta eat. He had just finished getting a second lid ready when he looked up and saw the approach of Weatherby.

"Ah, Weatherby," said Fat Jack, "What in hell brings you here?"

"I was passing through and saw all the cops," said Weatherby. "You guys attract cops like shit attracts flies. What's going on around here now?" Weatherby plopped his ass down on the bench.

"Nan stabbed Lester," said Fat Jack. It looks bad. The paramedics worked on him for quite a while, maybe twenty minutes, but they finally gave it up and covered him." Fat Jack tipped his beer and took a long and noisy glug. He set the can down with a bang and belched. "That crazy bitch really did it this time," he said, wiping his mouth with a filthy sleeve. "I guess we won't be seeing her around no more."

"That fuckin' Lester Rood needed a good killin' if you ask me," said Toby. "I'm surprised Nan didn't stomp a mud hole in his ass a long time ago. He was always knocking her around. Then not too long ago he stabbed her in the leg with that stupid screwdriver of his, you know, the one he sharpened and waved around all the time like it was Excalibur."

"I never did understand why she ran around with Lester," said Weatherby. "I thought she had more sense than that."

"They were a perfect match," said Toby. He was a pimp and a con artist and she was a sloppy drunk."

"Lester wasn't a pimp," said Weatherby. "That was all bullshit. Lester was just sadist." He poured some Franzia wine from the pouch in his pack into a plastic juice container. He took a long swig.

"*There is a crying for wine in the streets,*" recited Weatherby, "*All joy is darkened, the mirth of the land is gone.*"

"What in hell was that?"

"The Little Apocalypse of Isaiah," Weatherby said. Every time I come to this crazy park I feel like I'm in the middle of the fucking battle of Armageddon."

"The problem with you, Weatherby, is nobody ever knows what in the hell you're talking about," said Fat Jack. "You've obviously got too much time on your hands. You ought to get a job. All those fucking books of yours are turning your brain to mush."

"What books? All my shit got ripped off at the Sanctuary—my books, my dirty underwear, my toothbrush, everything."

"Who would want to rip you off, Weatherby?" Toby laughed, exposing his few remaining yellowed teeth. "You don't own anything worth a shit."

"How should I know? I woke up one morning and my stuff was gone. I looked everywhere, even the dumpsters. All I found was my empty pack. It was wet and smelled like piss."

"That's happened to me a time or two," said Fat Jack. "It has to be damn cold out before I'll spend a night in that fucking Sanctuary. Those assholes steal just to steal. Just for the hell of it. It doesn't matter what. Besides, the place has too many damn rules. A guy can hardly breathe. Yet everybody's shit always turns up missing and the goddamn staff is clueless."

Weatherby tapped out a cigarette from his pack and stuck it between his lips. "I need a light. Give me a light, Toby."

"Just use the damn fire like everybody else."

Weatherby grunted and ambled over to the fireplace. "Shit," he muttered, "I may as well be back in the stone age." Looking around on the ground for a small stick, he was abruptly taken aback at the sight of some sort of animal lying stiff and dead on the ground. Its brown fur was matted and filthy. It had a huge scaly tail. The face of the creature was contorted, frozen in an expression of incomprehension and torment. "What the fuck?"

"That's supper," said Toby.

"Supper? What is it?"

"You're about as dumb as a box of rocks, Weatherby," said Toby. "It's a damn beaver. Ain't you never seen a beaver before?"

"Yeah, on TV." said Weatherby. "The one I saw was alive, though. Where'd it come from?"

"The Fish and Game guys trapped it over at Logger Creek. It was gnawing down all the trees. I asked them for it and they gave it to me."

"You're not really going to eat that filthy thing, are you? Nobody's that crazy."

"Fuckin' A right, we're going to eat it," said Toby. "It's going to be one flavorful son of a bitch, too. I'll tell you what, beaver meat's good meat. I know people back home that'd give me 50 dollars for that very animal. Hell, back home, rib eye is dog food."

"You don't even know how long it's been dead. For all you know, it was dead in that trap for days before those Fish and Game knuckleheads found it."

"That doesn't matter. Beaver meat keeps. The pelt insulates it. Beaver pelts are valuable. I'll bet I could get 75 bucks for that pelt back home. They make hats out of it and such. I could even get money for the balls. They make medicine out of the balls. Cures gallstones and what not."

"A regular cash cow," said Weatherby.

"It ain't no damn cow but there sure is cash in it." said Toby. "You know me. I ain't one to sit around and watch the grass grow when there's money to be made."

"Yeah, you're some businessman, Toby," said Weatherby. "But you're not back in Arkansas and there's nobody around here who's going to buy that filthy animal. You couldn't even give the damn thing away."

"You know what your problem is, Weatherby? You got no brains and you got no ambition. All you do is drink wine and read those stupid books of yours. Poems, or whatever the fuck's in 'em. Jesus Christ, you ain't never going to get anywhere sitting on your ass reading poems."

"I know it," said Weatherby. "Hey, are you alright, Fat Jack?"

Fat Jack howled with pain as he pushed a palm hard against on side of his jaw. "This goddamn abscess," he said, panting. "I keep squeezing out puss, yet it keeps coming. Ugh. You've never tasted anything so foul until you taste the crud that comes out of a goddamn abscess."

Fat Jack had had problems with that tooth for years but he wouldn't go to a dentist, said dentists were against his religion. There was a time when he thought he'd fixed the problem. In a fit of pain and rage one day he had shoplifted a pair of vice grips, clamped the steel jaws over the tooth, and yanked until the blood spilled from his mouth. He managed to get the tooth out, but unfortunately it broke off, leaving the roots and a chronic abscess.

Weatherby stood looking down at the beaver. He nudged it several times with his foot. A rotten stench wafted up. "Jesus, what a stink," he said.

"What?" said Toby. "That beaver don't stink."

"Yeah, it does. Take a whiff of that, Fat Jack. It stinks, doesn't it?"

Fat Jack gave his jaw another hard squeeze and puckered, tasting the puss. He stood and walked the few steps over to the beaver. He stooped down and made a sour face. "Yeah, it stinks all right. It smells like crotch-rot. Whew!"

Toby walked over and took a deep sniff. His huge hairy nostrils flared. "Goddamn you, Weatherby," he said. "You ruined the meat."

"Get out of here. I didn't do anything."

Toby rolled the beaver over with the toe of his boot. A terrible smell rose from the carcass. "You did, you fucker. That meat is ruined."

"How'd I do that?"

"You kicked it."

"I didn't kick it. I just nudged it a little."

"Don't bullshit me, Weatherby, you dirty bastard. I saw you. You kicked it and busted up its guts. You ruined the meat. Now what the hell are we going to eat?"

"Go eat at the Sanctuary," said Weatherby. What's today? Wednesday? Wednesday is taco day. Their tacos aren't bad."

"Fuck that," said Fat Jack with a scowl. "I think it'll still be alright, Toby. We'll just have to cook the meat a little longer."

"Incinerate it, you mean," said Toby, shaking his head. "I like my meat rare, blood rare. I don't go in for that well-done shit. Well-done is for kids and people too dumb to know that the meat they're eatin' is as tough and tasteless as boot leather."

"Well, it's all we got and it'll still be better than taco day at the Sanctuary," said Fat Jack, giving Weatherby a dirty look. "So shut up and get to cutting, Toby. I'm about to starve to death. That fire's ready."

Weatherby thought it was an excellent time to leave. He said adios and grabbed his pack and half-filled juice bottle and headed over to the crime scene. The playground was only a few hundred yards from the fireplace, but the contrast between the two sections of the park could not have been more pronounced. The parkies had long ago realized the futility of trying to keep the fireplace area clean. Perhaps once a week they'd go in with rakes and shovels and haul away all the accumulated refuse. That was it. The playground was another story. The play equipment, benches and tables were all shiny and new. The shitters were freshly painted, the graffiti removed. The turf was a lush green, neatly mowed and trimmed, bordered with rows of petunias and marigolds.

The cops were in the process of interviewing all the witnesses. Most of these were little kids. Some kids chattered away, improvising elaborate nonsensical yarns. Others were more reticent and stood looking at their shoes. Getting even one or two words out of them was like pulling teeth. The cops looked weary.

Weatherby approached Police Officer Thornbeck. "Hey, Thorny," he said. "Another day in paradise."

"That it is," said Thornbeck. "Where've you been, Weatherby? I haven't seen you in months."

"I try to stay under the radar."

"Yeah? I heard you got an apartment and moved to suburbia."

"I did. I qualified for Section 8 housing and got a place over at Felony Flats."

"Well, what happened?"

"Same thing that always happens. I had it made and then I fucked it all up. They gave me the bums rush." Weatherby grinned, exposing his blackened craggy teeth.

"That's too bad, Weatherby. You back in the bush again?"

"Yeah. I was at the Sanctuary for a couple of weeks, but I split after all my stuff got ripped off. Besides, they have lice over there. I don't need that shit." Weatherby scratched himself and cringed at the thought of lice.

Next to the shitters a few feet away, Lester lay dead on the concrete. He was covered with an old canvas tarp and looked like a piece of wadded up trash. "Nan really did a job on that crazy Lester," Weatherby said.

"Yes, she did. Funny thing is she told me she'd do it. She told me the day I arrested Lester for stabbing her in the leg with that idiot screwdriver of his. She said if he ever tried anything like that again she'd take that screwdriver away from him and stick it up his ass. At the time I thought she was just drunk and rattling on."

"Nan usually kept her word. Did she use the screwdriver?"

"She did indeed. Well, to tell you the truth, I'm glad I

don't have to deal with that psychotic son of a bitch Lester anymore," said Thornbeck.

Nan was not far from Lester, kneeling on the grass next to a trash bin, her hands cuffed behind her back, a thin string of bloody drool snaking from her mouth onto the grass. Now and then she let out a low sustained growl and shook her head from side to side.

Nan never did look the part of a drunken vagrant. She was petit, weighing perhaps 90 pounds, and still rather pretty. The most notable thing about Nan Cherry, though, was her quiet demeanor. She didn't have the boisterous swagger and toothless bravado of the ordinary, run-of-the-mill park drunk.

Thornbeck rubbed the corners of his mouth with his thumb and forefinger. "It's a damn shame. There was always something about Nan. She didn't really belong out here. Do you know if she has any family?"

"Yeah, but they never have anything to do with her. Not even her kid."

"I didn't know she had a kid."

"Yeah, a son. He must be around 20 years old by now. It's a bizarre situation. Nan's son is at the same time her brother. Her father knocked her up when she was a teenager. I guess he was some kind of religious kook."

Thornbeck frowned and shook his head. He took off his glasses and wiped the lenses with a rumpled piece of Kleenex.

"Hey Thorny," Nan slurred, squinting in the bright spring sun. "Thorny!"

"Yes? What is it?" Thorny put his glasses back on and turned in her direction.

"I really need a beer. I feel terrible. I'm sick. Get me a beer, will you Thorny?" She tried to focus on Thornbeck's blurry image but gave it up and resumed staring at the ground.

"I think you've had enough already," said Thornbeck.

"You don't need another beer. You're already so drunk you don't even know it."

"No, I'm not. I'm not drunk. C'mon Thorny. Just one beer. I'll never ask you for anything again."

"Why don't you let her have a beer, Thorny?" Asked Weatherby. "The only brew she'll get from now on is pruno and that shit is as nasty as it gets. If she's lucky she might get a little raisin jack on feast days. '*In that day, sing ye unto her, A vineyard of red wine.*'"

"Don't be stupid, Weatherby," said Thornbeck. "Have you any idea of what would happen to me if I was to go and do a stupid thing like that? I'd be living here in the park, that's what, hanging out at the fireplace with Toby and Fat Jack— once I got out of jail, that is."

"Well, you'd be eating high on the hog," laughed Weatherby. "They're over there right now gutting and frying up an old rotten beaver carcass. Toby claims it's a delicacy back in Arkansas. That guy is one inbred country motherfucker, let me tell you."

"C'mon Thorny…," mumbled Nan. "I don't feel so good." Strands of her long dark hair were stuck to the perspiration on her wan face.

"Take it easy, Nan," said Thornbeck. "It won't be long now. Once I get you to the jail, they'll give you something to eat and a bed. You'll feel better once you get some sleep."

"Thanks, Thorny," Nan said. "You're a good friend." She blinked several times, wincing as if her bloodshot eyes were filled with sand. Then, as if hearing the call of a far off muezzin, she slowly lowered herself and plopped her face directly onto the damp turf.

Later in the afternoon, Weatherby sat on a bench smoking a cigarette and watching the children play. The young mothers, many of them pregnant, smiled and chatted breezily among themselves. The air was balmy and pleasant and carried an odor of lilacs.

A couple of magpies chased a young sparrow through the boughs of the trees above. The tiny sparrow was quick and agile and, for a brief moment, Weatherby thought it might escape the predators. But in the end it was no match for the two of them. The magpies chattered and screeched as they feasted. Weatherby hated spring.

THE HOLE IN THE TOILET PARTITION WASN'T
there the day before. It was lined with gray duct
tape, presumably to protect whatever was poked
through it from wood slivers. The strips of tape
stretched outward from the hole in all directions
like spokes around a wheel hub. It looked like a
crude mandala or roulette wheel. Scratched into
the paint near the hole was the image of a drip-
ping phallus and the word, Nirvana.

Swanson stood in the entry of the toilet
stall, packing a pinch of snuff behind his lower
lip. "Somebody carved out another one of those
stupid holes in here," he said. "They're drilling
these damn things faster than we can fix them."
He rubbed his hands together briskly to rid
them of the tobacco crumbs.

"Spring fever," said Swiveller. He scanned
the dank restroom. Faintly illuminated by the
dirty sky light, the blood streaks on the battle-
ship-gray walls appeared as some form of ancient writing. They zigzagged and crisscrossed
all over the aged and battered concrete blocks.
In places, the blood lines ended in a graceful
flourish, in others, an emphatic splat. The blood
on the pitted and uneven concrete floor had
collected into rivulets and pools amongst the
usual litter of beer cans, spent lottery tickets,
condoms, soiled clothing, puddles of vomit,
and what not. Swiveller imagined an orgy of
horrific violence. He winced as acid from his

LOOKING FOR NIRVANA

73

stomach rose up his esophagus. "Keep that crime scene tape up. Maybe it'll keep out the sightseers."

Swanson dragged the coiled water hose over near the sink and plopped it down on the floor. He screwed the end of the hose onto the spigot. "You don't look so good today, Swiveller."

"I'm alright," Swiveller said. "I didn't get much sleep. Maxine freaked out on my porch last night. I hadn't heard from her in several weeks so I thought things were cool. But then last night there she was pounding on the door and ringing the doorbell. There was no way I was letting her ass in. I told her through the door to beat it before I called the cops. That didn't do any good. She just stood out there pounding on the door, ringing the doorbell, calling me from her cell phone, and howling like a coyote. It was driving me nuts. I can only imagine what my neighbors were thinking. Finally she took off, yelling that she was coming back with a gun. Maybe 20 minutes later, she showed back up. She went right for my bedroom window. She tore off the screen, broke the glass, and started to crawl in. Fortunately the cops showed up when they did."

"No kidding. Did she have a gun?"

"No, that was bullshit."

"Yeah? What did the cops do?"

"Not much. They tried to talk to Maxine but all she would say to them was, 'You can't arrest me for love.' She kept saying that, over and over. It was weird. The cops asked me if I wanted to file a complaint. I said no. So they just told her to beat it and threatened to arrest her if she came back."

"What?" Swanson was incredulous. "She says she's going to go get a gun, she breaks into your house, and you just let her go? You're crazy, Swiveller."

"I've been trying to tell him that for years," interrupted a familiar reedy voice. Albino Jim had wandered in, his dirty hands wadding the crime scene tape into a ball. "What's the purpose of this bullshit tape?" he snorted. "This isn't going to keep anybody out."

Albino Jim had been around the parks for years, although nobody knew where he actually lived. He was as thin as a skeleton with skin the pallor of a bleached corpse. He ordinarily flitted about as silent as a phantom, and had a disconcerting way of suddenly appearing and just as suddenly disappearing.

"Apparently not, damn you, Jim," Swanson said. "And now that we're agreed on that, will you get the fuck out of here so we can get to work? Can't you see we're busy?"

"You guys are busy? That's a first." Albino Jim glanced around the room at the streaks and spatters of blood. "Man, what the hell happened in here?"

"A couple of punks got beat up and left for dead. I guess the Birdman found them early this morning and waved down a cop. As usual, we're stuck with the mess."

"That's pretty fucked up. It makes you wonder if it was real love. Or just another Saturday night." Albino Jim laughed at his own joke.

"My money's on real love," said Swiveller.

"I'll bet that son of a bitch Birdman had something to do with it," said Jim, wiping his nose with his shirt sleeve. "This looks like something he'd do."

"The Birdman?" said Swanson. "No way. The guy can hardly walk anymore. He sits all day everyday under that same Sycamore tree, drinking and shitting himself. I'm surprised he has the strength to lift a can of beer."

"Maybe so. But you'd be surprised what that mean son of a bitch can do. Hell, he's the one that threw me into the fire. You remember that, don't you?"

"Yeah," said Swiveller. "I remember. How's that leg?"

Albino Jim put down his pack and grocery sack of beer. He pulled up his filthy pant leg to reveal the large burn scar, a mottled discolored mess stretching from his knee to his ankle. "They had to graft skin from my stomach," he said.

"Put that thing away, will you?" said Swanson. He spit a long string of tobacco juice. It landed on an empty beer can with a ping. "It's goddamn repugnant. Christ, it smells. Is it still giving you pain?"

"Hell, yes." Jim pulled down the pant leg. "People see me stumbling around and think I'm drunk so they call Five-O. But I ain't drunk. It's just sometimes my leg hurts so bad I can barely walk."

"Why'd the Birdman throw you into the fire, Jim?" Swiveller asked as he worked at sweeping the debris into a large center pile.

"He claimed I was pawing his girlfriend's ass. I doubt that. I'm not much of a ladies' man. But then I was drunk. I don't remember. I don't even remember him throwing me in the fire. I sure as hell remember the pain afterwards, I can tell you that. It hurt like a motherfucker."

"I can imagine," Swanson said. "Anyway, where have you been, Jim? I haven't seen you in a while."

"Jail, man," said Jim. "I did two weeks."

"Yeah? What was the rap?"

"Drunk and disorderly, man. A group of bicyclists called Five-O and said I was drunk and camped out here in the shitter. That was all bullshit, man. Anybody who knows me knows I don't hang out in shitters. I go in and do my business and get out. I'm a business man. I've been a business man for 15 years. Besides, like I told Five-O when they showed up, I don't drink 211."

"What does drinking 211 have to do with anything?" asked Swanson.

"There were some empty 211 cans on the floor that the Five-O boys said were mine. Shit, you'd never catch me drinking that horse piss. Those were the Birdman's empties. Anyway, I finally had a belly full of those idiot bicyclists in colored spandex who think they're on the Tour de France. There must have been 20 of those fuckers and their bikes all crowded into the shitter at once. It was like being in the middle of a stampede. A guy can't even take a crap in peace anymore and I told them so. What do you clowns think this is, I said, a goddamned circus? It's ten in the morning on a weekday. Don't any of you bums have jobs? I guess that pissed them off."

Swiveller snorted contemptuously. "Yeah, Swanson and I deal with those pompous bastards all the time. You can't get anything done when they're around."

A tall bearded man with an enormous belly wearing red suspenders and a cowboy hat walked up and stood in the doorway, tapping a rolled up magazine on the jamb. "Is the shitter open for business?"

"What do you think?" said Swanson.

The man looked around the room and frowned. "I guess not. What the hell went on in here?"

"Good times run amok," said Swiveller. "It happens every now and then, especially this time of year."

"Kids go crazy during spring break," said Swanson.

"Why can't they go crazy somewhere else?" said the man. "This is damned inconvenient. I got business to take care of." He tapped the magazine several times into the palm of his hand.

"You can use the women's room," said Swiveller. "There's nobody in there."

"I can wait," said the man irritably. "I'll find somewhere else." He wedged the magazine into an armpit, grabbed a hold of his belt with both hands and tried to hitch up his pants. The attempt was futile due to his enormous overhanging belly.

"Do you guys like this kind of work?" he asked.

"Sure," said Swanson. "What's not to like?"

"There's never a dull moment," added Swiveller.

"You sons of bitches are crazy," said the man. He took one last look at the blood streaked walls, turned and walked away.

"We're crazy?" said Albino Jim. "That nut had on a belt and suspenders at the same time."

"So?"

"You can't trust a man who wears a belt and suspenders at the same time."

"Don't be ridiculous, Jim," said Swanson, spitting out a huge brown blob and wiping juice from his chin with his shirt sleeve. "Hey, did you know Swiveller's girlfriend tried to shoot him last night."

"No kidding?" Albino Jim eyeballed Swiveller with interest.

"Swanson's full of shit, Jim. Maxine didn't have a gun. I told him that. You ought to write for the tabloids Swanson." Swiveller leaned back against the wall wearily.

"She broke out his window and tried to climb in the house. Swiveller didn't even press charges, the dumb sap."

"What good would it do to have her arrested?" said Swiveller. "Besides, I felt bad enough as it was. Maxine's had a rough go of it. Like everybody else, she's just looking for a little nirvana."

"Well, she ain't going to find any nirvana with a neurotic prick like you, Swiveller," snorted Swanson.

"I know it," replied Swiveller.

Albino Jim was abruptly out the door and gone without as much an 'adios amigos,' which was his way.

It was mid afternoon before Swiveller and Swanson finished spraying out the restroom, wiping the fixtures, and mopping the floor. They emerged into the beautiful spring sunshine. The pleasant breeze smelled of lilac and carried the shouts and squeals of playing children.

Swiveller took a long drink from the water fountain and slumped down on a bench. "I'm not going to fix that stupid fuck hole today. I figure we can just leave it until somebody calls and complains."

"Good idea," said Swanson. "It's too nice a day."

"You fix one and another appears overnight. It's a waste of time."

They sat and watched the Birdman in the distance lying in the shade of an Elm tree, languidly tipping a can of beer.

THE WOODEN SHACK WAS THE ONLY BUILDING of the old slaughterhouse complex that hadn't either fallen down or been knocked down. It stood in a small clearing just to the west of Gut Creek, a channel that had once carried a stream of blood, urine, and intestines from the kill floor of the old slaughterhouse to a series of retaining pools near the river. Over the years the gore that had run down Gut Creek had fertilized the surrounding soil, resulting in immense towering thickets of willow, dogwood, sumac, and Russian olive that almost completely enclosed the clearing and the shack. It was isolated and, but for the pleasant racket of the birds, quiet. Rita Peckingcrow considered it a paradise of sorts.

Rita soaked a rag with peroxide and applied it to the wounds on Weatherby's ass.

"Hey, that hurts, damn you," Weatherby winced. He lay on his stomach on Rita's bedroll with his pants and shorts pulled down to his thighs. The shack had no windows and the light from the open door and Rita's oil lamp did little to brighten the semi darkness of the interior. The faint light splashed over Rita's pitted and scarred face. The socket of her left eye remained in deep shadow, like a crater on the far side of the moon. Her large muscled frame was clad in her usual flannel shirt, denim jeans, and heavy leather work boots.

The pleasant scent of damp and rotting leaves crept in through the door. Rita always kept the door ajar when she was up and about. She disliked the feeling of being closed in. She'd once done time in the penitentiary for gunning down her husband with a 12 gauge. The jury was sympathetic once they had a look at Rita's bruises and scars, and particularly her missing eyeball. Nevertheless, they convicted her of manslaughter and gave her ten years. She did six.

"Shut up and hold still cowboy," said Rita. She frowned and squinted with her one eye as she daubed peroxide onto the two small punctures, finding it difficult to work in the thick tangle of hair. "This is ridiculous. I've never seen so much hair."

"What do you want me to do about it, Rita?" Weatherby growled, reaching for his pack of non-filtered cigarettes. "Shave my ass?" He tapped out a smoke, stuck it in his mouth, and lit up.

"Alright, Winston, don't get excited." Rita smiled good-naturedly. "I'm just piling it on a little. A good shave couldn't hurt, though."

"Winston?" Dick Swiveller said, raising his eyebrows. "What's this 'Winston' shit?"

"That's my name, you dope. I'm Winston Burton Weatherby the Third. My dad was a general in the Pentagon. I have a pedigree."

"No kidding. I always thought you had just the one name, sort of like, you know, Madonna. You've been holding out on me. I've never heard you called anything but Weatherby. Winston Weatherby—sounds like the name of some country club golf hustler." Swiveller winked at Rita.

"Shut the fuck up, Swiveller, will you please?" Weatherby said, indignantly. "I could have been killed last night and all I get is ridicule. Just an inch or two over and Needle Bob would've skewered my asshole with that machete of his. Or worse, he'd have punctured my ball sack. That crazy son of a bitch."

"And here's the machete." Swiveller twiddled a Tom Mix pocket knife between his thumb and forefinger. It wasn't a genuine Tom Mix, just a cheap imitation you can find at any Five and Ten. "It looks about like the kind of knife Needle Bob would use," he said. "That idiot could fuck up a cup of coffee."

"All things considered I would imagine that Winston here is glad Needle Bob is such a fuck up." said Rita. She applied a final piece of tape to the bandage on Weatherby's hairy ass, picked up a half smoked cheroot from the ashtray next to the bed, and lit up.

"Do me a favor, Rita, and just call me Weatherby. If the name Winston gets around, I'll never hear the end of it. Country club golf hustler—fuck me."

"Alright, don't get excited," said Rita, puffing away at the cigar. "You know, I'm surprised Needle Bob's out of the joint so soon. I heard he got ten years, and here he's out on parole after just a few months."

"He did a 120-day rider," said Swiveller. "If violates his parole, he'll do the ten years. You and I both know that crazy bastard will be back in the joint before long."

"You're right, I reckon," said Rita. "You can pull up your pants now, Weatherby. That hairy ass is starting to gross me out. I don't know how long that bandage will hold with all that damn hair, but it's better than it was. You should have come over when it happened. Those wounds could have gotten infected."

"That's what I told him," said Swiveller. "He's stubborn. He hates going to the doctor. I had to bribe him with a box of wine to get him to come here."

"Damn right I hate it," said Weatherby. "It's humiliating, all that poking and prodding, all those jibes about me being too hairy. The only thing missing is the rectal thermometer my mother used when I was a kid."

With a good deal of grunting and straining, Weatherby

pulled up his pants. He turned over onto his back and did up his fly. He adjusted Rita's pillow under the nape of his neck and spit a fleck of tobacco from the end of his tongue.

"Lucky for you I don't have a rectal thermometer. I'd have used it whether it was called for or not," said Rita. She leaned back against the wall, her long black braids hanging past the pockets of her shirt.

Nearly every day at least one poor ailing son of a bitch braved the thickets and thorns to cross Gut Creek to be examined and treated by one-eyed Rita. She set bones, bandaged wounds, and prescribed remedies. Her treatments were more or less effective and the price was right. Since the money for Rita's medical supplies, as well as her food, tobacco, and other necessities, came from the sale of her birdhouses, she was happy to take wood scraps, nails, screws, glue, or paint as payment for her services.

Birdhouses in various stages of construction hung from the rafters and lined the wall opposite the bed. The birdhouses were intricately fashioned from odd scraps of wood and metal to resemble bungalows, train depots, barns (with tiny weathervanes), cathedrals, log cabins, and what not. Once completed, Rita sold them downtown at the farmer's market on Saturdays. Most sold for around 25 bucks, some for as much as 50—a pittance considering the amount of fuss and bother Rita put into their construction.

"You'll need to come back so I can change those bandages," Rita said to Weatherby. "Unless you can con someone else into changing them." She glanced meaningfully at Swiveller. Swiveller countered with a look of disgust. "And in the future, you might consider keeping your tongue in your head, or at the very least, watch where you wag it."

"Your ass," said Weatherby, annoyed. "There is a limit to the amount of speed-freak bullshit a normal person can listen to in a day. I mean he showed up at my park really flying, just all over the goddamned place, going on and on, telling me about this baby he has and these crazy fucking women he's involved with. What a sordid inbred country fucking drama that is. You remember that loony girlfriend of his, Donna Jo? Well, after she went to prison, Needle Bob started getting it on with her sister. Then *she* went to jail."

"Yeah, I remember," said Swiveller. "The last time I talked to him he told me all about how he was laying the pipe to the sister's daughter, Donna Jo's niece. As usual, he included a lot of stupid gratuitous details, like how she admired the size of his dick, how big her tits were, and how when she came, her spew flew across the room and splattered against the wall. Typical Needle Bob bullshit."

"You got it. Well, he knocked her up."

"Knocked who up?"

"The niece," said Weatherby. "She had the baby while Needle Bob was in prison. Now that he's out, Needle Bob wants the kid. Meth-crazed paternal instincts, I suppose. He got all misty-eyed when he showed me its picture. It was all so ridiculous I could hardly keep from laughing in his face."

"It was probably just as well that you didn't," said Rita.

"Yeah, I hear that. All I wanted to do was get as far away as possible from that raving nut. But, no dice. You know how Needle Bob is. He grabbed a hold of my arm and stuck that disgusting, sore-covered face of his just inches away from mine and started feeding me some shit about how he had killed a guy in the joint. Jeez, you should have smelled his breath—it was like a mixture of puke and something dead. Well, I had to ask him what the fuck he was doing out, if he killed a guy. He told me that the guy he killed was such a pain in the ass that the guards actually thanked Needle Bob for getting rid of him. That did it for me. I couldn't take anymore."

Weatherby took a deep breath, exhaled loudly, and stared at a birdhouse hanging from a rafter directly above him. It was freshly painted and fashioned to look like the gingerbread house out of Hansel and Gretel. Weatherby seemed hypnotized.

"Any day you want to finish the story," said Swiveller, "feel free to continue."

Weatherby turned to Swiveller and broke into a wide grin. "I told him to get the fuck away from me with that shit. I told him if bullshit were silver dollars, he'd be a fucking millionaire." With that, he roared with laughter which immediately set off a coughing fit.

"Take it easy, will you? You're about to have a heart attack. Here, drink some wine." Swiveller tossed Weatherby's dirty backpack onto the bed.

"Good idea," Weatherby said as the coughing subsided. From the pouch in his pack, he filled his sports bottle with wine, emptying it in one long guzzle. He filled the bottle again, smacking his lips. He looked a lot better.

"It's the resurrection," Rita said, "and we didn't even have to wait three days."

Weatherby and Swiveller prepared to leave and walked out into the crisp air. Rita followed. The three watched as flocks of finches and sparrows careened in high wide circles around the shack. Some came down to land in a loud flutter on the array of birdhouses that hung from the eaves of the old shack. The birds entered the tiny structures through doors and windows and emerged seconds later munching sunflower seeds, the husks drifting down and lighting on fallen red and yellow leaves.

A couple of birds squawked shrilly, dove down and lightly skimmed the top of Weatherby's head. Weatherby instinctively ducked, clasping his head in his hands. "You need to do something about these goddamned birds, Rita," he said, irritably. "Every time I come here, they dive bomb me. Those sons of bitches are killers."

"Stop being so melodramatic," Rita said. "They're just trying to keep the riff raff away." She laughed and lit a fresh cheroot, took a long drag, and exhaled a large cloud of smoke. "And speaking of riff raff, where do you suppose Needle Bob is holed up? I've got something for him."

"I imagine he's living in that rat's nest of his under the Americana Bridge," Swiveller said. "I see him almost every day hanging out with the drunks in Kootenai Park."

Rita disappeared inside the shack and reemerged moments later with the gingerbread house and a purple Crown Royal bag filled with seeds. "Give him this, will you? Tell him to put in the seed and hang it up somewhere. Birds are good company."

"You're both fucking nuts," snorted Weatherby. "Needle Bob is over the edge, man, he's fucking homicidal. He's not going to hang that stupid birdhouse. He's just going to hawk it and piss away the money, probably on drugs and machetes."

"I don't care," said Rita, puffing on her cigar. "What he does with it is his own business."

Rita stood smoking in the chilly air, watching Swiveller head down the path to Gut Creek with Weatherby skipping along close behind like a three-legged dog. They reached the creek and disappeared into the brambles. The slanting evening sun added a sparkling brilliance to the reds and yellows of the trees and a whitewash to the remaining timbers of the slaughterhouse. The birds were quiet. The beauty of color and silence, she thought. She turned and went into the shack.

Dick Swiveller sank heavily into the thickly padded mauve chair. The walls were the sticky pink color of cotton candy, adorned with the usual prints of ocean waves and chubby cheeked little girls in pastel pinafores holding flowers and colored balloons. He'd been reading his worn copy of *Naked Lunch* out in the lobby, and the holdover of those images in his mind made the décor seem even more nightmarish and hallucinatory. Numerous plaques hung in neat rows like bowling trophies—diplomas, licenses, awards, and what not, bestowed upon Ann Susan Baron, Master of Social Work. Another pop psychologist. Swiveller wasn't optimistic about his future.

"You've got mental problems," Hochstrasser had told him back at the cemetery office. "I made you an appointment with the shrink. This is your last chance. This is it. You done pissed the man off. You fuck this up and it's going to be your ass."

Swiveller shrugged and didn't reply. Hochstrasser was full of shit anyway, a clown whose fuckups were legendary. Like the time he sprayed the entire rose garden with herbicide, thinking he was applying fertilizer. Within a few weeks all six hundred rose bushes were black and dead. And then recently, Hochstrasser had "misplaced" two urns of ashes and ended up burying two identical urns filled with pea

THE COCONUT CHICK

89

gravel. Though the family was unaware of the substitution, Hochstrasser was still sweating that one.

Ann Baron, M.S.W., sat primly in a crisp Prussian blue pant suit directly across from Swiveller, reading from the chart on her lap. The prolonged silence made Swiveller ill at ease. Fortunately, Ann was nice to look at. She had to work at it, though. It was obvious she spent a lot of time and money on makeup, facials, creams, toners, soaps, electrolysis, surgeries and what not, in the futile attempt to mask the inevitable rot and decay of aging. Swiveller guessed her for a smoker, noticing the deepening furrows running up and down the pale skin around her mouth and into the red lipstick.

Ann reminded Swiveller vaguely of the lady that drove into the cemetery everyday in her shiny Lexus, ostensibly to visit a relative, but really to dump her empty booze bottles and related detritus into the cemetery cans. Curious, Swiveller had fished out the swag a few times. She drank expensive wines and liqueurs and apparently didn't want her trash collector to know she was a drunk. Swiveller had seen this sort of thing often enough. The interesting thing about this lady was her obsessive fastidiousness. She always carefully wrapped her red lipstick stained cigarette butts in paper towels, put tape around this neat little package and sealed it in a plastic sandwich bag. The bottles were each neatly wrapped in white butcher paper and banded with masking tape. Swiveller figured her for an addictions counselor.

"So," said Ann finally, looking up from the chart "how long have you been working at the cemetery."

"A couple of months. I used to work in the parks."

"Was that a promotion?"

"Hardly," laughed Swiveller. "The cemetery is the penal colony of the Parks Department. It's where they send you when you fuck up."

"What did you do to be sent to the cemetery?"

"I destroyed a barbeque grill."

"Why would you do a thing like that?"

"There is this tramp couple, Fern and Roy; they live in the back of Arcadia Park. They're pigs. I've been picking up after them for years. Anyway, one day I was cleaning out all their junk from along Spring Creek and I stepped in one of Fern's turds. It was disgusting. Have you ever stepped in human shit?"

"I have not," said Ann, frowning.

"It's not pretty and I was fucking pissed. Once I finished cleaning my boots, I hooked one end of a big chain to the back of the truck and the other end to the grill they always use, stepped on the gas and pulled that son of a bitch right out of the concrete. Completely destroyed it."

"Did that make you feel better?"

"Yes, it did," said Swiveller, nodding in satisfaction. "I felt wonderful."

"How might you have handled that situation differently, more productively?"

"I have no idea."

"Well, there were certainly negative consequences for your actions. You're now at the cemetery, which you consider to be a form of punishment."

"Yes."

"And you're still having difficulties. I read in your file that you suffer from depression and anxiety. Are you on any medications for that?"

"Yes."

"Do they help?"

"I suppose so. I still feel pretty unhinged most of the time but that's normal. I'm able to leave the house so I guess I'm doing alright."

"Perhaps not so well, judging by this latest incident at the cemetery."

Swiveller shook his head and frowned. "That was all just a big misunderstanding. People just overreacted."

"Overreacted?" said Ann, raising her eyebrows. "I was quite shocked when I read your supervisor's account of the incident, plus what the Spellman family wrote in their letter to the mayor. It claims you and your co-workers behaved disrespectfully towards their deceased aunt. You actually laughed at the corpse. Let me see, yes, here it is, you referred to her as the 'Coconut Chick.' And then there's the part that seems frankly criminal to me—you broke a finger off of the corpse. It's certainly easy to see why this incident is a major public relations disaster for the city."

"That's all true but there's a lot more to the story," said Swiveller. He was suddenly exhausted at the ridiculousness of it all. The entire episode had taken on the air of tabloid journalism. The struggle to counter all the bullshit had become increasingly futile. Still, he had to take a crack at it.

"First of all," began Swiveller, "the so-called 'Spellman Family' doesn't exist. In reality it is a couple of thirty-something assholes, cousins I guess, neither named Spellman but both conveniently U.S. attorneys, who wanted the body of an old great aunt—*her* name was Spellman and she'd been dead for 40 years—exhumed so they could get an expensive diamond ring off her finger. This 'family' wasn't even supposed to be around. It was agreed they would be at the cemetery but would not watch the actual exhumation. We had no idea they had snuck up on us and were hiding behind the Rose of Sharon bushes. And yes, we were clowning around. We see a lot of fucked up disgusting shit and having a little fun helps. I can't apologize for that. You'd do the same in our situation. Besides, and I probably shouldn't say this, but her face really did look like a Coconut, all brown and covered with thick hair."

"That's what I'm talking about. You don't appear to have a problem with being so callous about someone's deceased relative—someone who was once a living, breathing human being. I see that as a serious lack of empathy. The breaking of her finger demonstrates to me not only egregious carelessness, but a rather frightening and sociopathic disrespect."

"I couldn't get the damned thing off. It's like it was rusted on. God tried to get it off and he couldn't. So I tried again and that's when the whole finger just broke off."

"I beg your pardon."

"About what?"

"You said God tried to get it off. What do you mean by God?"

"Oh God, yeah, his name's really Gordon Orville Dean. We just call him God. You know, they're his initials."

Ann frowned as she held her pen in the middle with her thumb and forefinger, twiddling it up and down like a see saw.

"We also have a Jesus working there also," added Swiveller, "except you pronounce it 'hay-soos.' But that's neither here nor there."

Ann placed her hand to her to mouth to stifle a yawn. Her nails were sky blue and decorated with tiny rainbows. "Jesus and God working at a cemetery. You don't often hear about that sort of thing. Interesting."

"It's pronounced 'hay-soos," said Swiveller, "Yeah, they're interesting alright."

"How so?"

"They're both crazy. Take God, for instance. He's a born liar and lazy to boot. With a burial just a few hours off, he'll say he's already dug the hole and everything's ready to go. The funeral director arrives and discovers there's no hole. Somebody else has to dig it, and I mean pronto. When asked about it, God denies even knowing about the burial."

"I imagine that can make your job frustrating," said Ann.

"To put it mildly," said Swiveller. "Surreal is what it is. It's like you're in some weird alternate universe. I'm telling you, God works in bullshit the way great artists work in oils. For example, he claims he was in some top secret Special Forces unit in Vietnam, so secret that at the end of the war the government decided to kill all the participants. God claims he's the only one still alive. The government hit men are still after him but he doesn't use a computer keyboard so he stays off their radar. According to God the government tracks you by identifying your prints through computer keyboards. He's a nut."

"I want you to notice your reaction when you speak of this God, or Gordon," Ann said mildly, picking a piece of lint from her suit and rolling it between her fingers like a piece of congealed snot. "You become very animated. You seem to harbor a lot of resentment toward him. Perhaps there is something in yourself that you dislike and fear, something this co-worker triggers. How do you feel about your other co-workers?"

Swiveller snorted. Counselors never were the sharpest tools in the shed. "Well, there's Jesus. He's about as paranoid and stupid as God. He thinks that Jews control television and the newspapers and that everyone is brainwashed. Except himself, of course. Jesus knows the Truth because he listens to right-wing shock jocks and gospel programs on the radio."

"Jesus," Ann said, still pronouncing it incorrectly. "Is he Hispanic?"

"I suppose his ancestors were. Don't tell him that, though. He hates Hispanics. He hates all immigrants and foreigners. He thinks they all ought to be rounded up and shot. Naturally the other Hispanics at the cemetery think he's a *culo* and want nothing to do with him."

"Okay, well, again, I want to put the focus on you. I'd like to help you come up with some new strategies for dealing with your co-workers and the situations you confront. Your supervisor Mr. Hochstrasser is concerned about you, not only with regards to the broken finger situation, but your mental health in general."

"I'll admit I'm crazy," said Swiveller. "But Hochstrasser has no room to talk. He's done some pretty loony stuff over the years."

"Mr. Hochstrasser's behavior is not under discussion here."

"I suppose not," said Swiveller.

The game was up and Swiveller knew it. Hochstrasser's 'concern' for Swiveller was bullshit, an elaborate ploy to cover his own ass. After all, it was Hochstrasser himself who named the hairy brown corpse the "Coconut Chick." He even posed for a picture, pretending to pick his nose with the dead woman's blackened finger. Still, there was no point in mentioning any of that. No one could possibly believe such a thing. There was nothing for it but to take a few undeserved lumps and, as far as possible, put a good face on it.

The sentence Ann imposed upon Swiveller was even more draconian than he thought it would be. He had to see Ann twice a month for three months and attend a series of Sensitivity Training classes. Swiveller even had to pay for the classes himself. He wasn't sure if he'd just rather be exiled to the wastewater plant.

Once she was rid of Swiveller, Ann poured herself a large glass of Beaujolais, lit a cigarette and opened a window. The building was climate controlled but she needed some real air. She downed the wine and poured another. She looked out over the vast parking lot to the horizon where the far away mountains met the sky in a haze of blue. The only thing she knew was that when she died she hoped her body was never found.

The mallards swam lazily in the waters of the secondary clarifiers. The mechanical arm, extending from the center tower to the edge of the circular pool, rotated slowly around like an hour hand, spraying a steady stream of water.

From the primaries across the access road, Leroy Two Dogs paused from skimming and watched the mallards. Waves of heat distorted the image of the floating ducks, making them appear misshapen and monstrous. "Did you ever notice that this hell hole is a goddamned nature preserve?" he said. He removed his hat and wiped the copious sweat from his tanned and leathery face. He took a long pull on his cigarette and flipped the butt into the foul water. The butt bobbed about next to an enormous fluorescent-blue condom floating languidly in the muck.

"Yeah, that's some jelly fish," said Simon the Leper, pointing to the condom. "It's a Portuguese Man o' War. Those things are deadly. They're worse than rattlesnakes."

No ducks swam in the primaries. The surface of the water was a pulpy mess of jellyfish, bloated brown tampons, known to the trade as sewer mice, decomposing parakeets, finches, and other small pets, toys, hypodermic needles, blobs of grease, and an endless variety of seeds. It was the job of the scruds to regularly skim the debris from the surface. The scruds were definitely at the bottom of the heap.

A GUY'S GOTTA HAVE FRIENDS

"Mr. Crumb fished a 50 dollar bill out of here day before yesterday," said Two Dogs, pulling on the lever that tipped the edge of a half pipe below the surface of the water, allowing the watery gunk to flow down the pipe and into a vault.

"What did he do, dive in?" asked Simon.

"No, nothing that dramatic," laughed Two Dogs. "He just stood here and waited for the money to float down. Once the bill got to the half pipe he snatched it out of the water, blew the seeds and the rest of the crap off of it, and put it in his shirt pocket."

"It's amazing he never gets sick," said Simon, scratching at the fish-like scales that covered his face. Afflicted with a rare skin disorder since birth, Simon the Leper looked as if someone had glued hundreds of small tile shards onto his skin and then filled the cracks with bright red grout. He reached into a pocket of his baggy, dirty coveralls and pulled out a pint of bourbon. Looking around him furtively, he took a long swig and wiped his dribbling mouth with a filthy sleeve. He extended the bottle to Two Dogs.

"Hey, not so obvious, Man," said Two Dogs. "There's Seamays."

"Where?"

"Over there, by the digester, walking around with that big dog turd in his mouth." Don Seamays was the plant manager. He constantly prowled the plant smoking long, fat banker cigars. "The last thing I need now is to get busted for drinking on the job. Seamays is a righteous dude but I know he'd sack me for drinking and man would my parole officer have a shit fit. She'd have me back in the joint for sure."

"I hear that. I was lucky Seamays even hired me in the first place. I don't want to press my luck. Hey, look at this." Simon donned a pair of rubber gloves, reached down and pulled the object from the muck.

"What in the world is that?"

"It looks like some sort of weird bird." Simon flicked off

some of the debris. "Hey, it's one of those prehistoric birds like you see in the cartoons. I forget what you call them."

"Well, I'll be dipped in shit," said Two Dogs. "It's a ptero-dactyl. I thought I'd seen everything. Man, I'm glad these crazy bastards aren't still flying around. There wouldn't be any of us left." He flicked at the tiny plastic claws with his forefinger.

"Let's give it to Mr. Crumb. He can add it to his col-lection."

"Alright. I don't know where he's going to put it, though. He's running out of shelf space."

"Not anymore," said Simon. "He put up some new shelves. He'll like that prehistoric bird. He always lights up like a little kid at Christmas when he finds a new critter."

"Yeah, and he talks to the damn things," said Two Dogs, putting the pterodactyl in his pocket. "The other day, I walked in on him and there he was talking shop to a little plastic army man, what they did in the war, that sort of horseshit."

"Well, I imagine if you were shut up in the septage building all day you'd be talking to plastic army men, too. I don't know how he does it. It smells terrible in there, worse than shit."

"He could always prop open the door, let a little fresh air in. He never does, though." Two Dogs swatted away a fly that had landed on his forearm and briskly rubbed the skin. A large tattoo of a grinning skeleton hanging from a gibbet covered the forearm. The lines were sloppy and uneven, a jailhouse tattoo.

"I think he feels like it's the one place in the world where people can't fuck with him."

"Yeah, probably so," said Two Dogs. "He's not much for being social."

"I can understand that," said Simon.

Two Dogs pushed open the heavy steel door of the septage building and he and Simon entered the close and evil-smelling gloom. Mr. Wilbur Crumb stood next to the clanking machinery doing a pH test. "Ah, house guests," he said with a grin, exposing a set of rotten, jagged teeth. Wilbur Crumb was pushing 70. He was frail, flabby around the middle, and bony everywhere else. The machinery he operated filtered the waste trucked in from suburban septic tanks. The waste was heavily concentrated and much worse than anything that came in through the sewers. It was whitish, thick, stringy, and lumpy, like rancid cottage cheese or vomit. A large cylindrical screen rotated towards Mr. Crumb, carrying with it the usual jellyfish, sewer mice, wads of matted hair, decomposing hamsters, toys, electronic remote controllers, and what not. A large rectangular blade chopped loudly at the mess as it came over. Freshly severed chunks plopped into a trough. The stench was indescribable.

"What are you guys doing, slumming again?" Mr. Crumb squinted and held the pH test strip up to the light. "You know, if my old friend Don Seamays catches you in here, it's gonna be your asses." He laughed.

"Yeah? So what else is new?" said Two Dogs. "Goddamn, it's foul in here. I can hardly breathe. How can you stand to be in here all day long?"

"I guess I'm used to it. Besides, there are worse places." With a shaky hand, the old man wrote the pH number on a thick plastic bag, filled the bag with a sample of the viscous ochre-colored liquid and sealed it. He chucked the bag at Simon. "Make yourself useful. Put that in the freezer, will you please?"

Simon walked over to the freezer, opened the grimy door, and tossed in the bag. Next to the freezer was Mr. Crumb's swivel chair and work table. The table top was a mess of rumpled papers, magazines and tools. His battered clock radio was tuned to his favorite easy-listening lounge-music station.

"Anyone who had a heart
Would take me in his arms and love me, too
You couldn't really have a heart and hurt me,
Like you hurt me and be so untrue"

100

"You ought to change the station on that radio once in a while, Mr. Crumb," said Simon. "Give yourself a little variety. Take a walk on the wild side."

"I don't take walks," cracked the old man, grinning and rubbing his gnarled, arthritic hands together. "Besides, that radio only has one station."

"So I've heard." Two Dogs pulled the pterodactyl from his pocket. "We found this in one of the primaries, thought maybe you could add it to your collection." He passed the pterodactyl to Mr. Crumb.

"Hey, well ain't that something," said the old man as he examined the plastic figurine. "I've never seen one of these before. Sure has a lot of nice detail." He tottered over to the shelves where he kept his collection. On display were the hundreds of toy figurines he had fished out of the sewage over the years, among them cartoon characters, aliens, spacemen, cowboys, Indians, dogs, horses, monsters, and creatures of the sea. Though he had given them a good scrubbing under the water spigot, they remained discolored and filthy. Many were missing heads and limbs. Mr. Crumb placed the pterodactyl next to the Creature from the Black Lagoon.

"It's the toy store from hell," said Two Dogs. "How long have you been collecting these crazy things?"

"I don't know, thirty, thirty-five years," said Mr. Crumb. "They've been good friends. It's pretty lonely in here most of the time. It can make you crazy. A guy needs someone to talk to. A guy's gotta have friends."

The door opened abruptly and in walked Seamays, puffing on his big cigar. "What's going on here?" he said, glancing about the room. Nobody said anything. "Nothing's going on here," said Seamays, answering his own question. "Simon and Two Dogs, I thought you two were supposed to be hosing off those aeration basins."

"We were just on our way over there, Don," said Simon. He and Two Dogs turned and headed for the door.

"Glad to hear it," said Seamays. "I thought for a minute there that you two were in here fuckin' the dog. I'm glad I was wrong. Anyway, be careful on those basins. I don't want anybody falling in. And I don't want to see any more drinking. This ain't no country club."

"Okay, boss," said Two Dogs as he followed Simon out into the hot sunlight.

The door banged shut and Seamays sniffed the close foul air with a grimace. "Well, how are things, Mr. Crumb?"

"I'm a little down in my back, but I guess I'll live," wheezed the old man. "Where've you been, Don? I don't see much of you anymore."

"I've been around. They keep me pretty busy these days."

Mr. Crumb tottered over to a chair and sat down. Seamays struck a match on the concrete block wall and relit his cigar. He turned toward the door.

"Come back when you can sit a while," said Mr. Crumb.

"Will do," said Seamays.

The milky brown water in the aeration basin churned and roiled. It lapped at the smooth concrete sides, leaving a layer of scummy foam. Two Dogs and Simon the Leper stood leaning on the iron railing that surrounded the basin spraying jets of water from hoses at the foam stuck to the sides. The layers of foamy build up sloughed slowly off.

"Mr. Crumb told me he fell in one of these aeration basins a long time ago," said Simon the Leper over the steady whining roar of the blower motors.

"Bullshit," said Two Dogs. "You fall in there, you ain't coming out. That water's had so much air pumped into it, it has no buoyancy. You can't swim in it. You just sink down to the bottom and choke to death on aerated ass water." He shuddered at the thought.

"I know all that. But Mr. Crumb says he didn't get out. He doesn't think he did, anyway."

"What the hell does that mean?"

"How should I know? I'm just repeating what he told me. He said he fell in and nobody else was around and he doesn't think he got pulled out, at least he doesn't remember getting pulled out. He thinks he died then."

"That old man's lost his mind."

"I suppose you're right. Strange things do happen now and then, though, things nobody can explain. Like the other day I was at the grocery store and this little girl walked up with a bag of candy and she offered me a piece. That had to be one of the weirdest things that have ever happened to me. I mean, it really freaked me out."

"What's so unusual about some dopey kid offering you a piece of candy?"

"My face, dummy. It scares people, especially little kids. They think I'm a monster. I don't blame them; I know I look like a monster. When I'm in public I always keep my eyes on the floor and try to be as invisible as possible. That little girl who offered me the candy was the first person who has ever approached me. She startled me, let me tell you."

"I can imagine," said Two Dogs. "The world seems to get weirder and weirder all the time."

Once they had finished hosing down the basins, Simon pulled the pint from his pocket, took a hit, and passed it to Two Dogs. Two Dogs took a pull and slowly screwed the cap back on. A blue heron flapped its giant wings high over the inferno of asphalt and concrete. Two Dogs and Simon watched it until it disappeared over the cottonwoods that lined the river.

THE TRUCK AND TRAILER HAD APPEARED in the parking lot of Nez Perce Park sometime in the early morning, dropping from the sky like the *Santa Casa di Loreto.* Or so it seemed.

Dick Swiveller walked around the rig. The trailer, and the truck that pulled it, were parked parallel to the curbing, taking up the whole damn parking lot. Both the truck and the trailer had recently been painted with what appeared to be latex house paint smeared on with a sponge. The paint was blobbed, streaked and swirled, the truck battleship gray and the trailer dark green. Underneath the curtained window next to the door was a Day-Glo orange peace sign.

Bamboo Tiki lights were pounded into the grass in front of the trailer. They formed a circular perimeter around a display of 15 or 20 chainsaw carvings—bears, fish, wolves, mountain lions, and what not. A variety of dreamcatchers hung from nails driven into the trees. All items were tagged and ready for sale.

Swiveller could hear the occupant inside creaking about, mumbling and belching. Abruptly from the rear of the trailer a steady stream of bluish-brown liquid began to spatter on the asphalt, a heavy stream, like a racehorse pissing on a flat rock. He smelled the foul odor of sewage.

Swiveller retrieved the spill kit from his truck and pulled out a few 4-foot absorbing socks. He placed the socks around the perimeter of the growing puddle to keep the sewage away from the storm drains. He walked around the trailer and rapped on the rickety warped door.

No response.

Swiveller rapped again.

"Who is it and what do you want?" said a voice from inside.

"Parks Department."

"So?"

"So you just emptied your septic tank onto the pavement."

"The door swung open. A small, middle-aged man stood running a comb through his hair. He was bald on the crown of his freckled head. The thin, gray hair sprouting from the sides and rear was scraggly, hanging past his shoulders. He wore a Guatemalan long sleeved shirt made from flour sacks. His tie-dyed pants were baggy and held up by a drawstring. He wore no shoes.

Though it had been many years Swiveller immediately recognized Oswald Moody. Moody was at one time Swiveller's A. A. sponsor He was the last person on earth Swiveller wanted to see.

"Well, if it isn't Dick Swiveller," said Moody. "I figured you for dead. Damn your eyes, you interrupted my meditation. What's with the costume?"

"Hello Oz. You mean the shirt? I work for the parks department."

"The parks will hire just about anybody." Moody laughed.

"Lucky for me," said Swiveller. "I needed a job."

Moody rubbed his eyes with his hands, blinked several times and said solemnly, "The reality is you actually don't need a job. Like I told you many times, working for a living is not living."

"Yeah, I remember."

"I heard you went back to drinking."

"I did for a while. But I've been off the stuff for a long time now."

Moody eyed Swiveller doubtfully. "How can that be? I haven't seen you at any meetings."

"That's because I don't go to them anymore. I haven't been to an A. A. meeting in ten years or better."

"Obviously you're on a dry drunk then," said Moody, wrinkling his brow. "You're not working a program and I'm guessing you're still on the meds too."

"Well, you know what they say, better living through chemicals," said Swiveller dryly.

"Well, I've said it before and I'll say it again—it doesn't matter if you drink it, smoke it, pop it, or stick it up your ass, it's all the same thing."

"Whatever, Oz," said Swiveller. "Let's get to the issue at hand. You just emptied your septic tank onto the pavement."

"That's a problem?"

Swiveller sighed. "Yeah, it's a problem. You have several gallons of raw sewage trying to make its way to the storm drains. I've got it contained but it's going to take a while to clean up."

Moody stepped out of the trailer and he and Swiveller walked around the back.

"That's dishwater, Swiveller."

"Take a whiff of it," Swiveller said. "It smells like shit to me. Anyway the blue toilet chemical gives it away. Not that it really makes any difference what you dumped. The fish in the river don't like dishwater anymore than they like sewage. So I think it would be a good idea for you to just pack up and leave."

"How is that a good idea?"

"Because I know you don't have the money for the fine you'll have to pay if I get the cops over here. You and I were once friends. I'm giving you the chance to just get the hell out here."

"Fine for what? Dumping dishwater?"

"Dumping anything. You can't do it. You also can't camp overnight, sell your sculptures, drive nails into the trees, and whatever else you've been doing here. This is a public park, not your own personal flea market or carnival."

"You know, Swiveller, you sound like a goddamn traffic cop. You can't do this and you can't do that. I don't know if I ever told you before, but you have a maximum security prison right between your fuckin' ears."

"Yeah, you told me. Many times. Just do me a favor and start packing. What do you say?"

"I say it's all beautiful, Dick," Moody said. "I'll move on. We'll do your trip."

"Beautiful," said Swiveller. He pulled an armload of absorbent pads from the spill kit and laid them into the puddle. The pads immediately began to expand and curl into a variety of grotesque shapes.

Swiveller walked over and sat down at a picnic table in the shade of the giant elm. He watched Moody load sculptures into the bed of his old pickup and waited for the absorbent pads to do their work. A figure approached from across the parking lot. It wasn't until the figure spoke that Swiveller recognized him.

"It's Dick Swiveller unbound," said Weatherby. "Returned from exile at last. And properly penitent, I hope."

Swiveller laughed. "I didn't recognize you, Weatherby. With those clean clothes and new shoes I thought you were a Mormon missionary looking for his lost bicycle. What happened to your beard?"

The skin where Weatherby's beard had been was a pale grayish yellow and spotted with angry red bumps. "It's one crazy story," he said. "But first, you need to get the raccoons out of the dumpster. It's No-Ears and her brood."

"Again? I figured she learned better after the last time. Alright, I'll get her out."

"What's all that about?" asked Weatherby, gesturing towards the truck and trailer.

"You'll never guess. It's Oswald Moody. He's leaving."

"Really? The Bhagwan? From the A. A. days? Get the fuck out of here."

"None other."

"What's that terrible smell?" said Weatherby, his face contorted in disgust.

"He emptied his septic tank on the pavement, the dope."

"Sounds like something the Bhagwan would do." Weatherby walked over and stood at the edge of the fetid, brackish pool. *"By the rivers of Babylon we sat down and wept when we remembered Zion,"* he said.

Moody heaved the final sculpture—a brown bear with a salmon in its mouth—into the back of the truck and wiped the sweat from his face with his sleeve. "Must be Weatherby," he said. "Sure sounds like his bullshit. I thought by now you'd be dead for sure."

"Almost, but not quite," said Weatherby.

"What happened to the tan and the Speedo?" said Moody. "You used to look like a beach bum. Now you just look like a bum. You look sick. I'll bet you haven't screwed the cap back on that wine bottle in ages."

"I don't drink wine from a bottle," replied Weatherby. He raised his Gatorade bottle to Moody. "A toast to you, Baba Sahib."

"You're about a crazy motherfucker, Weatherby. I'm guessing that's not Gatorade."

"You've guessed correctly. Nobody in their right mind drinks Gatorade." Weatherby walked back to the table.

"Weatherby, I'm going to get No-Ears out of the dumpster. Are you coming along?"

"No, I'm going to sit and rest my dogs, maybe have a little chin wag with the Bhagwan here. I'm tired. I walked all the way from Castle Rock this morning."

Swiveller fetched a ladder from his rig and headed for the dumpster. Peering into the empty container he saw the raccoons pacing back and forth and scratching at the metal sides. It was No-Ears and her litter all right.

"Don't worry, little mama," Swiveller said. "I'll have you out of there in no time."

No-Ears looked up at Swiveller and pawed at the slick metal. The raccoon had been around for several years. Swiveller had no idea if she was simply born without ears or lost them in a fight. He preferred to think it was the former. He didn't want to think about No-Ears getting her head chewed by a pit-bull in a spiked collar belonging to some meathead.

Swiveller placed the ladder in the dumpster, leaning it upright against the inside lip. One by one the raccoons crawled up the ladder and dropped out on the grass. Once free, the raccoons hesitated, sniffing the air and looking at Swiveller.

"Well, don't just stand there," said Swiveller. "Beat it. You're free."

Swiveller watched as the raccoons disappeared into the woods. He was partial to the raccoons. No-Ears and her many litters had been good company over the years.

Moody was pulling out of the parking lot by the time Swiveller got back. With the pickup bed overflowing with animal sculptures and the little green trailer bringing up the rear, Moody's rig looked like a crazy circus train.

"Keep your nose clean, Oz," Swiveller said. He waved. Moody waved back and gunned the engine, leaving a cloud of black exhaust.

Swiveller checked the spill. The pads had absorbed all the liquid. With a square point shovel, Swiveller scooped the sopping mess into two giant red bio-hazard bags. He tied up the ends, hauled them across the lot and tossed them into the dumpster.

"It's like it never happened," said Swiveller with satisfaction upon his return.

"It still stinks," said Weatherby. He took a big drag on his unfiltered cigarette.

"What do you want from me?" said Swiveller. "The reality is all you have to do is decide that it smells wonderful and it will."

They cracked up at that.

"Speaking of the Bhagwan," said Weatherby, "he left this." Weatherby handed the card to Swiveller. It was a business card illustrated with pictures of buckskinned Native Americans and various dreamcatchers. 'Oswald J. Moody' it read. 'Mystic, Shaman, Teacher, and Ordained Minister of the Church of the Galactic Dreamcatcher. Available for Weddings and Baptisms and Counseling. Reasonable Rates.'

"That's it? I figured Moody would really give you the business."

"Not too bad, surprisingly," said Weatherby. "He just told me the reality is I was going to end up in jail, a nuthouse, or dead if I kept on. He told me to call him. I suspect he wants me join up with the circus again."

Swiveller studied the business card. "Moody always said he wanted to start his own religion," he said. "You know, he even had his own holy writ; this manuscript he wrote himself called 'The Gift of the Wand.' It was assigned reading, a ridiculous book filled with pseudo-Native American wisdom horseshit. I don't know which was worse, the book or Moody's interminable monologues. Still, it beat having the Big Book rammed down my throat by some sadistic psychopath on parole."

Weatherby laughed. "Like Wes?"

"Yeah, like Wes," said Swiveller. "What made you pick that sick motherfucker?"

"I didn't. I refused to get a sponsor so my P. O. picked one for me. Just my luck he picked Wes. What a fucking asshole. He wasn't my sponsor for long, though. One night at a meeting he confessed to the group that he'd once been so drunk and horny that he'd fucked a little kid, raped her, and had gotten away with it. I remember he went into a lot of detail, really sickening. It was like he was proud of it or something. I wanted to gun him down like a dog. I fired him the next day."

"Well, if you want to move up the food chain in A. A., you need good stories and lots of them—the more sordid and disgusting the better. Look at Wes. He was definitely the kingpin of the Grapevine Club. I imagine he went ballistic when you fired him."

"He did. He was immediately on the phone to my P. O. and told him I wasn't working the program. My P. O. violated me and I went back to jail."

"Nice guy."

"No shit."

"So tell me, what happened to the beard? It must have taken a chainsaw to get that fucker off. And you're wearing clean clothes. That's not like you. In fact, it's weird. Give."

"Well," Weatherby said, "yesterday I wasn't feeling so well. I was lonely and depressed and feeling sorry for myself, thinking about life and how I fucked things up, thinking about my dead son, friends I used to have, my old dog Ernie, that sort of thing. Anyway, there I was, sitting at the table drinking my wine, minding my own business, trying to cheer myself up with a little reading when these people from a party across the way brought me over a hot dog and a couple of beers. You know I don't drink beer, but I didn't want to be rude, so I asked them to put the beer on ice for me. That was a polite way of handling that, don't you think?

"Sure. Will you get to the main part?"

"Will you keep your shorts on?" Weatherby emptied the Gatorade bottle, belched and continued: "We talked for a while and they went back to their party. A couple of hours later, two of them came over and said they were going to hook me up, that they'd gotten me a hotel room and a fresh change of clothes. I wasn't too sure about it all you know. I thought maybe they wanted to take me off somewhere, roll me, and light me on fire. But you only live once, I thought, so what the hell, I went along."

"So where'd you go? The Ralfroy? Kitchenette and free cable?"

"No, not that swanky," Weatherby said with a black-toothed grin. "I don't remember the name of the joint but it was definitely upscale—and a real fucking trip. Must have cost a fortune. Every room had a different theme. I got the Tropical Paradise room. The shower was a rock waterfall and the bathtub was a pool surrounded by palm trees. The bed was up in a tree. I had to climb these stairs made of rope to get to the damn thing. The walls were all painted in murals depicting vast oceans and islands and clouds. It was beautiful, man."

"I've never heard of such a thing," said Swiveller.

"Neither had I. Of course nothing was real but I didn't give a shit. There was this basket next to the waterfall shower that had everything: razors, shampoo, cologne, clean clothes, and lots of good wine. I hadn't had a bath or slept in a bed in months. The bath was great. I must have soaked in it for two hours, drinking wine. I couldn't sleep, though. I'm not used to a bed. Besides, I've always been suspicious of paradise. I got up around four and beat it out of there."

"Who were these crazy people?"

"I have no idea," said Weatherby. "Never saw them before in my life. Just ordinary people doing somebody a good turn for the hell of it, I suppose."

"They don't sound very ordinary to me."

"Well, maybe not," Weatherby said. "You know, it occurred to me as I was watching the Bhagwan pulling out of the park with his funky little trailer and all those weird animals that I missed my calling. I mean, the dude has got it all. He's the ringmaster of his own crazy circus, he camps where he pleases, he's fawned over by young women, and he gets paid for talking nonsense."

"Well, as Moody always said, 'Thought creates form.' All you have to do is visualize it and poof! It appears."

"All you have to do is believe your own bullshit, you mean," said Weatherby. The problem with me is I've always felt like those raccoons trapped in the empty dumpster, expecting at any moment to be buried in a ton of sewage and trash. And the only ladder around is the imaginary one." He refilled the Gatorade bottle from the wine pouch in his pack. "The Bhagwan was right about one thing, though. I am dying."

"I know," said Swiveller.

"The doctor told me my liver is shot and my next drink was going to be my last. What was that, a month ago?" Weatherby coughed, took a good swig and lit a cigarette. "But I'll tell you, Swiveller, I'm ready. I'm tired, man. I'm ready for some peace and quiet. *He came all so stille where his mother was, As dew in Aprille that falleth on the grass.* It's either going to happen on its own or I'm going to make it happen, the sooner the better. Thought you should know."

Swiveller stared down at the grass, momentarily transfixed. "It's alright, I don't blame you." he said finally. "You've done your best, man."

Swiveller walked over to where Moody's setup had been. He picked up the scattered bits of twine, the Styrofoam packing peanuts and the cigarette butts. He fetched a claw hammer and pulled the nails from the trees. A faint odor of shit remained.

**"I FIGURED YOU GUYS WERE BACK," SAID** Dick Swiveller. "Somebody took a shit in the urinal."

"No more than you deserve," said Fern Stone-Jones, looking up from her stained and tattered Bible and sneering at Swiveller. Fern and her common law husband Roy Flowers sat at one of the four picnic tables affixed to the concrete pad in the meadow between Spring Creek and Arcadia Pond. As always, the table and surrounding area were cluttered with clothing, stuffed animals, opened tins and plastic deli containers of half-eaten food, bicycle parts, beer cans, Fern's discarded adult diapers, and other debris.

Fern and Roy had been living on and off along the banks of Spring Creek at the back of Arcadia Park for years. Arcadia Park was a nature preserve in the heart of the city, a habitat for deer, blue herons, red-wing blackbirds, Canada geese, swans, and so on. The primary visitors to the park were birdwatchers and lumpy white-haired retirees wearing loud, florid polyesters and walking old graying dachshunds. Needless to say, Fern and Roy were as out of place in Arcadia Park as turds in a punchbowl.

Fern tipped her can and swallowed a huge hit of beer, belched loudly and turned to Roy. "Roll me up a smoke Roy Boy. Fuckin' Swiveller makes me nervous."

YOU DON'T LIVE HERE

Roy dutifully put down his newspaper and retrieved a plastic produce sack containing dirty snipe tobacco from his pack. He rolled, licked and twisted the cigarette with his blackened fingers and then placed its entire length in his mouth and slowly drew it out again. He handed the smudged and soggy cigarette to Fern.

Fern took it and lit up. She reached across the table and patted Roy's gaunt and bearded face. "You're a goddamn saint, Roy Boy," she said, the cigarette dangling from her lower lip. Her bloodshot eyes floated like oysters in a pool of cocktail sauce.

"It's alright, honey," said Roy, reaching out and squeezing her hand. Despite their odd appearance and filthy ways, Fern and Roy weren't all that different from other middle-aged couples.

"What happened to your hair?" said Swiveller. Fern's head was completely shaved and dotted here and there with warts and scabs.

"Lice," replied Fern. "Since we've been out we've been staying nights at the Sanctuary. Some asshole took all our stuff while we were gone." She glanced sharply at Swiveller. "Anyway, some skank from St. Louis brought in lice. All the women had to have their heads shaved."

"Sorry to hear that," said Swiveller, nabbing beer cans and other debris and tossing it into a plastic sack. He was careful where he stepped.

"That's true, you're one sorry asshole. Well, it won't be long before you're really sorry. Obviously, you forgot I'm a Methodist. This world's gonna come to an end before you know it, motherfucker, and Roy and me are gonna be par-tyin' with Jesus. Not you, though, you evil bastard. Your ass is going to be on fire." Fern picked up a pink plastic lighter and sparked it, moving her hand in a circular motion just above the tiny flame. "And I'm going to personally light those flames."

"I guess that means you're not going to kill me and burn my house down," said Swiveller. Fern had been threatening Swiveller with murder and arson for years.

"I'm getting too old for that sort of thing," she replied mildly, spitting out a chunk of tobacco and flipping her cigarette butt onto the concrete. She sucked at the brown nicotine-stained tips of her thumb and forefinger. "Besides, assholes fuck themselves."

"I'm just doing my job," said Swiveller. "Somebody's got to pick up after you two."

"Yeah, and it's the devil's own work," said Fern.

"How so?"

Fern was indignant. "How about for setting the cops on us? Because of your lies me and Roy Boy had to do 52 days in jail."

"You guys were sawing up the tree branches for firewood. I told you more than once to cut that bullshit out."

"We didn't saw up any wood. All we used was the dead stuff we found lying around."

"Come off it, Fern. You two were busted red-handed with a saw and about a half cord of freshly cut wood stacked up alongside the grill."

"Bullshit," said Fern. "And that's another thing. You took out our grill. You're always ripping us off."

"This is a public park, a nature preserve. It's not your fucking house. You can't just leave your shit lying about. You two don't live here."

"So you always say," said Fern, with a wry grin. "*For the evildoers shall be destroyed, but those who wait for the LORD shall inherit the land.*"

"Okay, Fern," said Swiveller, weary of this exchange. He resumed his work picking trash. Arguing with Fern was like arguing with the sphinx.

Fern tipped her can of beer and glugged down what remained. She tossed the empty can onto the grass, hoisted herself from the chair and tottered over to the edge of Arcadia Pond. With mincing steps she slowly turned her entire body left to right and back again, as if surveying her kingdom. A large shit stain ran down the seat of her filthy green surgical scrubs. It looked like a vestigial tail.

THE OLD VAN HAD SEEN BETTER DAYS. FOR decades it had sat just off the alley behind the Campbell place, covered in layers of dust, bird shit and mud. There wasn't much chrome left on the wheels, just dirt and rust. All four tires were flat and crumbling. The orange flames on the sides were still faintly visible, though most of the black paint on the exterior of the van had long since oxidized into a flaky whitish gray.

"So, what do you think of my new pad?" asked Weatherby, eyeing Swiveller through the open side door. He lay on the grimy red shag carpeting that covered the floor of the van. His back was propped up with tattered throw pillows and he was snug up to his neck under an electric blanket.

"Nice," said Dick Swiveller, seated on a rickety lawn chair just outside in the sunlight. "Mag wheels and flames—what more could you ask for?"

"Nothing," said Weatherby. "I got it all—TV, lights, heat, the works. Otis Ray really hooked me up. There ain't nothing that old guy can't do."

The skin on Weatherby's face was a sickly, dirty yellow color and was drawn tightly over his cheek bones. He took a last drag on a hand-rolled cigarette and butted it out, blowing out an enormous cloud of smoke.

"That's cool of Otis Ray and Edna to let you stay here."

"Yeah, no shit," said Weatherby. "Just in time, too. My belly and legs are swollen so damn bad I can barely walk."

"Looks like this van's been here a while."

"Since 1975," said Weatherby. "Otis Ray told me it once belonged to his son, Robert. Robert died at 22 and Otis Ray never moved it from the spot where Robert last parked it."

Swiveller shook his head. "What happened to Robert?"

"Otis Ray didn't say." Weatherby lit another sloppy-looking, hand-rolled cigarette and spit a chunk of tobacco from the end of his tongue. "I'd give anything for a decent cigarette. These Prince Albert roll-your-owns are nasty."

"What are you doing smoking Otis Ray's tobacco anyway, you mooch?" Swiveller said with a laugh.

"Hey, he told me I could help myself," said Weatherby. "Besides, it's all I have. I'm broke."

"I suppose you're drinking his beer, too," said Swiveller.

"Oh, come off it. You know I don't drink beer. Besides, a six pack of beer lasts Otis Ray a week or better. And that's when he's on a drunk."

"Are you still off the wine?"

"Definitely. I'm too damn sick to drink it. Hell, I can hardly keep anything down."

"It's strange you not being in the park anymore. I don't find Franzia wine boxes in the trash cans," said Swiveller, squinting and blinking in the bright cold haze. "All I find are dog turds wrapped up in little plastic baggies and cups of half-drank latte. Dog shit and lattes—that's what we've come to. And then there's this goddamn sunlight. Two weeks before Christmas and it's the same piss-yellow hazy light, day after day, week after week. No rain, no snow—nothing. It's depressing."

"How's the breathing?" asked Weatherby.

"It sucks," said Swiveller. "It's always hard to breathe this time of year."

The temperature inversion had settled into the valley in October, trapping the freezing cold air, along with all the wood smoke and car exhaust of the city. The tree tops and the nearby foothills were hidden in the haze. "No matter how many times I hit the inhaler, I feel like I'm being squeezed in a vice. I'm sore all over."

"Speaking of being squeezed, I suppose you heard they found Albino Jim," Weatherby said. He shuddered.

"Yeah, in Salt Lake City," Swiveller said. "He told me once he'd never be caught dead in Salt Lake City. Yet, there he was."

Once the weather turned cold Albino Jim always climbed the fence at Pacific Recycling and slept in the piles of cardboard. One morning he somehow ended up in the crusher. Some dock workers in Salt Lake unloading a truck noticed a lot of blood on one of the pallets. They cut the bands and pulled apart the compacted bale of cardboard and discovered what remained of Albino Jim.

"I hope he never came to. I'd hate to think he woke up in the crusher."

"No shit," said Swiveller. "What a horror."

Neither said anything for a time. Swiveller puffed his inhaler and munched on a stick of Trident. Weatherby chain smoked, occasionally pulling back the blanket to gently rub his swollen legs. The door to the back of the house opened and out bounded Fred. He headed for the sycamore tree, lifted his leg and pissed. Spying Weatherby and Swiveller, he trotted over, tail wagging, and hopped up into the van.

"Fred's a cool old dog," said Weatherby, running his fingers through the heavy white fur. "He keeps me company out here."

Otis Ray Campbell emerged from the house and hobbled over to the van. He was rail thin and stoop shouldered. He wore a heavily mended pair of country bib overalls and a ratty felt fedora. As always, a hand-rolled cigarette dangled from the corner of his mouth. He pulled a can of Coors from a pocket in the overalls, and popped it open.

"How're you doing, Otis Ray?" said Swiveller. "I haven't seen you and Edna in the park for a while."

"I've been having troubles getting around lately," Otis Ray said, sipping the beer. "Damn knees are killing me. Fred's been itching to go, but I just haven't been up to it. How's the Parks Department treating you, Dick?"

"It's okay," replied Swiveller.

A window at the rear of the house slid open and a female voice said loudly, "Daddy, are you boozing it again?"

Otis Ray was in the middle of a long sip. "No," he said, bringing down the can. He winked at Swiveller.

"Well, tell Winston I'll be out in a minute with his pills."

"I hear you, Edna," said Weatherby, but she'd already closed the window.

"Winston. I always get a kick out of that," said Swiveller. "What a ridiculous name."

"Shut up, Dick. I can't help it if I have blue blood."

"Speaking of which, when was the last time you talked to the general?"

"I don't know—years."

"Who is the general?" Otis Ray wanted to know.

"My father," said Weatherby. "We don't get along too well. He's convinced I'm possessed by a demon. Like most military officers, he's big into demonology."

Swiveller smiled at that. "Is he still at the Pentagon?"

"I imagine so."

Edna emerged from the house carrying a tray. She was a tough-looking, stringy old woman in a gingham dress. Since she hadn't put her teeth in—she rarely did—her chin nearly reached her nose when she talked, ate or just chewed her cud. "How're you doing, honey?" she said, approaching the van. "Are you feeling any better?"

"No, I'm feeling a little worse," said Weatherby. "I'm about to keel over, I'm afraid."

"Nonsense, son," said Otis Ray. "You just passed a bad waterhole somewhere. A couple more weeks and you'll be up and around, good as new."

"That's right," said Edna. She set the tray down on the shag carpeting. From the tray she selected several ominously large pill bottles and tapped a couple of pills from each into a dosing cup. She handed Weatherby the cup along with a glass of water.

Weatherby dumped the pills into his mouth, took a sip of water, tipped back his head and swallowed them down. "Thanks Edna."

"I sure wish you'd come stay in the house," she said. "I think you'd get better a lot quicker. It's cold out here and getting colder."

"You're a sweetheart, Edna, but I'm doing okay. I've lived outdoors for so long, this van is about as close to inside as I want to get."

Edna pulled a cover from a bowl and steam rose up in swirls to the tattered and stained fabric hanging from the ceiling of the van. "Well, okay," she said. "Here's some oatmeal. You're supposed to eat something with those pills and besides, you're not eating enough as it is.

"Bless your heart, Edna, I'm doing my best."

"I know, honey. Well, you two have a nice visit. I'll send Daddy out later to get the tray and check on you. Nice to see you, Dick."

Otis Ray and Edna went back in the house. Otis Ray called for Fred, but the dog didn't budge from Weatherby's side.

"Does that crazy dog stay out here all the time?" asked Swiveller.

"Most of the time," said Weatherby, scratching the dog's head. "It gets a little cramped in here at night, but I'm glad he's around."

"Why don't you just move into the house?" said Swiveller.

"I tried, man. But after years in the bush, a guy just can't go to living in a house all at once. Edna keeps it hot as hell in there. And there's the constant racket. Edna listens to these redneck gospels preachers on the radio in the kitchen and Otis Ray watches Three's Company reruns on cable in the living room. I think he gets off on watching those two chicks in hot pants. It's hilarious. Naturally, that drives Edna crazy so she cranks up the volume on her radio and he responds by turning up the volume on the TV. And so it goes. Psychological warfare at its finest. What a madhouse."

Weatherby grimaced and struggled to find a comfortable position. Each position seemed to bring new and different pains and each time he moved Fred had to readjust, which made Weatherby want to move again. After a few minutes of futile effort, Weatherby gave up.

"You know, things are so different now, it's bewildering. I feel like I've been exiled, marooned on some strange planet. Though it's only a block down the alley from my old place at Castle Rock, it might as well be a million miles. I'm stuck here waiting, just waiting for something to happen. I feel like Major Tom, that guy in the David Bowie song:

'*For here*
*Am I sitting in a tin can.*
*Far above the world,*
*Planet Earth is Blue*
*And there's nothing I can do.*'"

Weatherby gazed off in the direction of the foothills. Cigarette smoke swirled about his head.

"I wish I could see those hills," he said. "Living in the park, I was right at the base of them. Now they're all shrouded in muck."

"I know what you mean," said Swiveller. "I wish it would snow, rain, hail—any goddamn thing."

"Jesus, I'm tired all of a sudden," said Weatherby with a deep sigh. "One minute I'm fine, the next I'm completely exhausted. Go figure. Well, I guess it's time for a little snooze."

Swiveller rose to go. "I'll be around tomorrow. Anything I can pick up for you?"

"How about a pack of smokes? Old Gold non-filters.

"You got it."

******

Not long after Weatherby died, the snow finally came. Huge flakes fell until the snow was a foot deep. The wind blew the snow into an alien landscape of drifts and eddies. Running the trash route, Swiveller, imagined himself as the last man on earth. At each stop he left the warmth of the truck, and with pockets stuffed with plastic bags, trudged through the new snow collecting the trash. Now and then a ghostlike form walking a dog would suddenly emerge from the white, bundled and hooded, and just as quickly vanish. Otherwise, the parks were deserted.

It was afternoon when he climbed the snowy rise next to the ancient abandoned armory on his way to the new can. It was some three hundred yards away from the nearest path at the northern edge of the park. Swiveller had been ordered to place the can in such a remote location because one particular patron had complained that his dog always shit in that particular spot and he wanted a can there, as well as a shit sack dispenser. The park patrons were always a pain in the ass. Swiveller didn't mind servicing this particular can, however. The route there and back took him past Weatherby's old spruce tree.

Approaching the tree, Swiveller noticed movement in the branches and heard a muttering human voice. He dropped the bags in the snow and parted the boughs. In the large open space at the base of the tree sat an unkempt man with a bottle of booze in one hand and a cigarette in the other cursing no one in particular.

"Willy Weird Beard," said Swiveller. "What in hell are you doing here?"

Willy looked up, startled. "Shit Swiveller, you shouldn't sneak up on a fellow like that. I thought for a second you were a cop."

Willy had put down the bottle and was tugging obsessively on the course hairs of his beard. Willy Weird Beard didn't have much of a normal beard, just a few sparse patches of fine soft light hair that grew an inch if that. On his right cheek near the corner of his mouth, however, he had a giant mole, perhaps an inch around, from which grew a thick lock of wiry dark hair. Willy rarely if ever shaved, so the hair from the mole was usually four or five inches long.

"I haven't seen you in months, Willy," said Swiveller. "Are you camping here now?"

"Sure. I moved in a week ago," Willy replied. "I figured I'd grab this place before somebody else did. What did you do, Swiveller, piss yourself?

Swiveller glanced down at his wet pant legs and frowned. "No I had a leaky bag. Goddamn dog shit and lattes. That's my life these days."

"Nice," said Willy with his toothy grin. "You know, this park is sure strange without Weatherby around. It feels like a goddamn cemetery. Where's he buried, anyhow?"

"He's not, at least that I know of," Swiveller said. "The general—his father—had him cremated and shipped back east. What the general did with the ashes is anybody's guess. He's not buried at Arlington, I can tell you that."

"Weird," mused Willy, chewing on his lock of beard. "One day you're here, the next you're completely gone, nothing left of you."

"Tell me about it," said Swiveller, picking up the bags. The snow was a milky brown where the bags had sat. "Well, I guess I'll be seeing you around, Willy. You'll like it here. It's quiet."

"Good. That's just what I'm looking for—peace and quiet. It'll be a good place to retire."

Swiveller headed back. He held the two bags as far out from his body as he could. By the time he got back to the truck his arms ached from the weight. Dog shit is heavy, like a sack full of mud. He heaved the bags in the back. They landed with a wet-sounding thud.

Swiveller sat in the cab of the truck with the engine running trying to breathe. His airway was squeezed tight and his lips and eyelids buzzed from the lack of oxygen. He puffed on his inhaler and listened to Perry Como sing "There's No Place like Home for the Holidays." Beyond that, there was nothing he could do.

He waited.

"**Well, if it ain't the sheriff,**" said the bearded man wearing a red Santa hat with white trim and little silver bells attached to the pom-pom. He was stirring some thick brownish muck in a pot over an open fire. "Game's up, I guess. Kind of a weird looking sheriff, though. Where's your gun?"

"I'm not a meathead," said Dick Swiveller. "I don't carry guns. I work for the parks."

"That's even worse." The man put a lid on the pot and stood up. "You'll run me off and then you'll tear my house down. Insult to injury. A guy's up against it in this world, what with all you boy scouts running around fucking up people's shit. A fine way to treat folks."

Sitting on a narrow strip of sand, cotton-woods and willows in the river near the north bank, the shanty was accessible only by a gi-ant snag that had years before fallen across the swift channel separating the small island from the river bank. The island was littered with logs and debris heaped by powerful river water into twisted, splintered grotesque shapes, frozen and covered with a blanket of virgin snow. The only civilization visible through the wooded jumble was the garish orange concrete and steel of the Taco Bell Arena.

Swiveller studied the shanty's construc-tion. It was a fortress of driftwood lashed to-gether with odd bits of rope and vegetation, the cracks packed with old clothing and mud. The walls and ceiling were at least a foot thick. He peered inside. Aside from a rime of dust covering everything, the interior was neat and orderly. To the right was Roddy's neatly made bed. Roddy had cobbled together a series of shelves upon which his clothes were folded in neat stacks. On the wall opposite the door he displayed his small library, tattered and dirty copies of *East of Eden*, *High on Gold*, *Inside the Mind of Ian Brady*, *The Bad Boys of Butte* and a few others. They were arranged not by category or alphabetically but precisely according to height, from tall to short. Spread out on the table to Swiveller's left was a half-finished jigsaw puzzle, a photo of a covered bridge in a colorful New England fall. On all the unused wall space Roddy had tacked up the completed puzzles he'd mounted and glued onto a paper backing. All the puzzles were beautiful photographs of craggy mountains topped with snow, trees, deep blue lakes, old barns, ghost towns, and the like.

"You're crazy if you think I'm going to rip this thing down," Swiveller said finally. "I'd be here till fucking Epiphany. What do you do during the spring runoff? This place is underwater in May and June."

"I sure as hell don't stay here. I bug out for higher ground. "*When the levee breaks, got no place to stay*," he sang, adding an affected and mellifluous "Oh Ho" at the end.

"That's a pretty fine Robert Plant imitation," said Swiveller.

"You like that? Years of practice." He shivered, pulled his Santa hat down to just above his eyebrows, and lit a cigarette.

"Looks like a warm hat."

"It's not."

"What's it for, then?"

Exhaling a cloud of smoke, the man hung the cigarette from his lips and pressed a dirty green button on the white hat band. Colored lights flashed around the band, and the pom-pom leapt up and began flapping from side to side ring-

ing the little bells as the hat sang Away in a Manger in a rau-
cous tinny voice.

"The thing's loud. Can't you turn it down?"

"No volume control," said the man loudly. "Gives you a
headache after a while."

The pom-pom finally stopped dancing, the lights blinked
off and the hat fell silent.

"It it makes you sick why do you wear it?"

"The holidays give me the blues. The hat kind of liv-
ens things up a bit. It's the contrast, I guess, like electroshock
therapy. Once the current is turned off, you feel better. Not
because the shock did anything for you. You're just not being
zapped anymore. The definition of paradise. "

He laughed as he tipped a can of Stack beer and glugged
down a few mouthfuls.

"Some nut downtown gave me the hat and offered me
15 bucks to wear it into this gay bar on Idaho Street, find a
dude named Diamond and say I had a message for him from
Lester, turn on the hat and do a little dance. So I did. Diamond immediately got this look on his face like he wanted
to kill somebody and stomped out. The bartender, though,
got a kick out of the performance. He poured me a few on
the house."

"That's funny the Diamond dude got pissed. I wonder
what that was all about."

"This hat pisses people off for some reason. Anyway,
who cares? I got 15 bucks, free drinks and I got to keep the
hat." He abruptly gave Swiveller a second take. "I know you."

"That so?"

"C'mon man, don't play Mickey the Dunce. Don't you
remember? We grew up together, same street, same schools,
everything. I'm Roddy Karado, man."

"Bullshit, Roddy Karado's doing life in the joint."

"Nope. Ugly rumors, man. I only got 30 years. My
brother Randy, he got life."

131

"Roddy Karado. I wouldn't have known you. Must be the beard, or that stupid hat. I remember the broken nose though. That was one bloody sucker punch."

Roddy rubbed his nose at the memory, leaving a dark smudge. He and Swiveller were smoking a bowl of dope at lunchtime in junior high when a strutting macho jock with a blond afro named Manwaring, without saying a word, walked up and sucker punched Roddy in the face. Broke his nose. No reason. Just for the hell of it.

"Ah, fond memories of the past," said Roddy. "I wonder what happened to that motherfucker Manwaring."

"He's a lawyer."

"You're kidding me."

"Hell no. You didn't think he'd end up a low-life working for the parks department, did you? His dad was a lawyer."

Roddy looked at Swiveller and smiled. "Well, you never know."

"I run into him now and again. He's fat and bald. You wouldn't recognize him. He's always glad to see me and acts like I'm his best friend, which is weird since he hated me in school. He seems lonely. He's usually half drunk and always has a story. He's either getting divorced or getting married to some chick, the love of his life naturally. His ex-wives are all bitches. He has five kids and the child support is killing him. He'll go on and on if you let him."

Roddy laughed. "Families are a nightmare."

"I know it," said Swiveller.

Swiveller lived three houses down from the Karado family. Roddy, the youngest and then Randy. Jo, their sister, was the oldest. Roddy's mom Doris was either sitting on the couch smoking Pall Malls and talking on the telephone or at the Elks lodge drinking beer and playing bingo. Now and then Mr. Karado would come stumbling down the gravel road from the Little Dutch Garden tavern rip-roaring drunk and boss everybody around for a while and make a pot of oxtail soup before heading back to the tavern. Swiveller always had to get lost for a while.

"I ain't feedin' no goddamn neighbor kids," Mr. Karado always said.

"So, when did they parole you?"

"No parole. They don't parole evil motherfuckers. I did my 30 year bit and not one day less. Got out a free man in 07.

"You are an evil motherfucker. I invite you to some major keg action up at Grimes creek but instead you and that sick bastard brother of yours rob and murder old Horst. What the hell was that about?"

"We just went to rip him off while he was taking a nap. But he woke up and started yelling so Randy smothered him with a pillow."

Swiveller shook his head in disgust. "I heard you idiots got forty bucks out of the deal. Some haul."

"Forty bucks and a 30-year bit in the joint," said Roddy, picking a piece of grit from the corner of his eye. "Seemed like a good idea at the time."

Old Horst lived one street over from Roddy and Swiveller. His was the first house built in the neighborhood. He built it himself after emigrating from Germany in the 1930s. The house stood only about 4 feet tall, just a row of windows and a roof. The rest was underground. To get to Horst's front door, you had to wade through waist-high grass and weeds and descend a flight of crumbling concrete steps.

Inside, the house was cluttered with junk—newspapers, phonebooks, crates of milk bottles, cardboard boxes, paper grocery sacks, coffee tins. Horst kept everything. You got from one room to another through a maze of interconnecting tunnels. The only place relatively free of junk was the area between the sofa and the television. On the walls hung faded photographs of Horst's relatives and just over the black and white television set Horst displayed the Iron Cross Second Class he'd received for valor in World War I. Horst had some

20-odd cats, their stench inside the house was rancid and overpowering.

In spite of the odor, Horst's house was a favored destination of the neighborhood kids. The tunnels were creepy and mysterious. It was amazing the stuff you might find, a rusted rifle, a box filled with old fishing tackle, an antique telephone, even a World War I-era army snake bite kit never used. Horst's place was better than the dump and if you asked he'd let you have most anything.

"You can haf it," he would say, always adding, "You kidz ah krrazcy."

Not everyone asked, however. Randy Karado was always robbing old Horst. Once he even swiped Horst's Iron Cross. Jo beat his butt and made him give it back. Still, Horst never barred Randy from the house.

"I guess Randy's still out at the joint," said Swiveller.

"No, he's been dead for years."

"That right?"

"Yeah, another inmate beat him to death. Days later, they were still finding pieces of Randy's skull. Randy snuck into the dude's cell and ripped off a picture of his daughter."

"Jesus. What the hell did he want with a picture of some guy's kid?"

"Anybody's guess. I imagine he whacked off to it."

"That sick idiot fuck," said Swiveller with disgust. He had always steered clear of Randy. Randy had the dead cold-blooded eyes of a shark. For kicks he tortured and killed small animals in gruesome ways. He also enjoyed starting fires. Once he doused Mr. Robertson's next door tool shed with gasoline and put a match to it. In his hurry to burn the building down he'd unknowingly spilled some of the gasoline down the front of his pants. He ended up with third-degree burns. Both legs were horribly scarred, and that only made him more vicious.

"There was definitely something wrong with him," said

Roddy grimly, seated on a log and tapping the long ash from his cigarette onto a dirty pant leg and rubbing it in.

"Do you remember him throwing darts and sticking them in your head?" Swiveller chuckled.

"Yeah, very funny. How could I forget? You're one to talk, though. You tried to murder me that time I blew pot smoke in your cat's face."

"I told you and everybody else a million times not to fuck with my cat. But you're not telling the whole story. You shot me with a pellet gun, you bastard. My mom had a hell of a time digging out those pellets."

"What did you expect? You were coming after me. A guy's gotta defend himself."

"Ah shit, I was just going to clout you one. You had it coming. But once you shot me that was it."

"You got yours, though. My sister slapped the shit out of you."

"That she did, the bitch. At least she didn't hold me down and shove ice cubes up my ass, like she used to do to you and Randy." Swiveller let out a loud guffaw.

"No shit. What a drag," said Roddy. "Jo was such a tyrant. Sometimes I hated her so bad I'd make these elaborate plans to kill her in her sleep. But I always chickened out. I was sure she'd wake up and catch me. Then it really would have been my ass. Funny thing, though—she was the only person who ever wrote to me in prison. Everybody else ignored my letters. They all came back marked refused."

"What did you expect you fucking bastard? Horst was a cool old dude. I wouldn't have written to your stupid ass."

"I guess I wouldn't have written me either," said Roddy ruefully. "I've tried to come to terms with the murder over the years, but no go. There's simply no excuse for that kind of bullshit. This crazy do-it-yourself preacher at the joint was always rattling on about how we're forgiven by the blood of Jesus. What hooey. You can never take something like that back.

Once you kill a harmless old man you're forever marooned in a dark alien place. It's too late. Like that Black Sabbath song:

"*Welcome to forever.*

*Welcome, it's too late.*"

"You know," continued Roddy, "there was this ongoing debate in the Letters to the Editor section of the newspaper during the trial. People were arguing over who would burn in hell longer, Randy and I or Hitler."

"I remember. You don't believe in that sort of stupidity, do you?"

"I don't know. I sure wish I hadn't missed that party, though."

"Ah, you didn't miss much. Typical kegger—a bunch of drunken and drugged fools standing around a bonfire for two days talking shit and listening to *Wang Dang Sweet Poontang*. The only real entertainment was watching Jack Harlan. He got so fucked up he could barely stand and was leaning against this tree and right in front of everybody pulled his pants down to his knees, grabbed his dick and let out this enormous stream of piss. It was hilarious. And then he just stood there motionless for hours like a catatonic leaning against that tree and staring off into space with his pants down and his dick in his hand. One chick, Kim Chambliss or somebody, even hung her coat on his shoulder like he was a coat rack."

"Jack was out at the joint a couple of times. I said hey to him now and then."

"Yeah, I heard he went up. Did you see Randy much after the murder?"

"Not once. They kept us separated at the joint. Hell, I was in seg for five years. Sometime in the early 80s Jo wrote and told me they'd transferred Randy to one of those super max outfits and not long after that he was killed."

"How is Jo?"

"I don't know. About 10 years ago the letters stopped. I never did learn what became of her."

Roddy stoked the fire and pulled the lid off the pot. He stirred the barely bubbling mixture. He dipped in a dirty gnarled finger and licked it. "Damn, if that ain't the best stew in town." He smacked his lips. "You ready to eat Swiveller?"

"Nothing for me, thanks. I had a big breakfast."

"Bullshit," said Roddy, ladling the brown glop into a filthy Disneyland souvenir mug. "When somebody offers you something, you take it."

As a kid, you always heard that phrase when you refused your go at the bong. It didn't matter if you were already too fucked up. *When somebody offers you something you take it.* He accepted the mug steaming with the viscous mixture. The rim was encrusted with blackened saliva and lip-crumbs. But there was nothing for it so Swiveller grabbed the sticky spoon and wolfed down the evil-tasting swill. Like most food cooked over an open fire and served on a frozen day, the stew was burnt and piss-warm at the same time. Roddy had obviously added all the ingredients at the same time. The celery and other vegetables had been cooked into a stringy slime. Swiveller got it down, burped and handed back the empty mug.

"Big breakfast my ass," said Roddy. "You inhaled that stew."

"Well, it hit the spot." Swiveller smacked his lips in disgust and stood up to leave.

"If I come home from work and find my house gone," said Roddy, "I'll know who to come gunning for."

"I already told you I'm not tearing the damn thing down. It's built like a brick shithouse. However, If the cops find it, that's another story. But I doubt you have to worry about that. You're pretty well hidden in here."

"*You* found it."

"I saw the smoke. Actually I didn't know if it was smoke or river mist. Keep that hat quiet and you'll be alright.

Swiveller carefully worked his way back across the old snag. He weaved in and out of the brittle branches, grasping them tightly. The trunk was treacherous. It had long since been denuded of bark and was slick with snow and ice. Below, a channel gurgled in and around snow-covered boulders and debris. He reached the bank and climbed the steep bluff to the road. Faintly, he could hear the Santa hat singing to the ringing of the bells.

*"I miss the earth so much*
*I miss my wife*
*It's lonely out in space*
*On such a timeless flight"*

**MEL GRINER SPAT A STRING OF BROWN** tobacco juice into the large E-Z Mart Styrofoam coffee cup adorned with green holly leaves and bright red berries. He picked a fleck of snuff from his tongue, rolled it in his meaty fingers and flicked it onto the mud-stained gray carpet. He licked his fingers and frowned.

"I've seen this coming. You just don't have that necessary level of commitment."

"That's not it," said Dick Swiveller. "I'm just sick of picking up after every thrill-seeking pig motherfucker in the city. It's gotten to the point where I dread nice weather."

"It's what you signed on for."

"Not exactly."

Griner put down the cup and picked up another exactly like it, this one half full of lukewarm coffee. He sipped, smacking his big blubbery lips. Griner was a giant of a man, well over three hundred pounds. With his pear-shaped skull, closely cropped hair and wide double chin he reminded Swiveller of General Burkhalter on Hogan's Heroes.

"Regardless, you got paid. As a matter of fact, you were paid well."

"Yes, I was. And I paid my dues. Thirteen years worth of trash, vomit, shit—you name it."

"What's this 'dues' business? This ain't a Shriners' convention. This is life. Life is short and then you die. It is what it is."

It is what it is. A cliché Swiveller particularly hated. Griner's favorite.

"You've been seeing that shrink for the past couple of years. What does she say about you quitting your job?"

"Nothing, really. Anytime I want to talk about the job and how sordid and degrading it is, she always steers the conversation to crap like 'thinking errors' and 'cognitive strategies.' 'Decide how you're going to feel.' Horseshit like that. "

"What are you going to do now?"

"I don't know."

"Well, if you don't know, no one else does either." Griner thought that was funny for some reason. He broke into guffaws, wheezing and snorting like a donkey. Swiveller remembered a time, years before, when Griner was genuinely funny. Back then he was just an ordinary gravedigger who pounded down two six packs of beer and pint of whisky every night. And every workday morning he'd launch straight-faced into a sardonic and hysterically funny monologue about the previous night's exploits. You laughed so hard your guts hurt.

"Have you been watching The Curse of Oak Island?" Griner changed the subject.

"No."

"You don't know what you're missing. It's exciting shit. There's some sort of treasure buried in this deep pit on the island. People have been trying to dig it up for the past couple hundred years. One expedition managed to excavate the pit down to 90 feet. On the way down, about every ten feet, they discovered layers of logs and at the bottom they found coconut leaves and a huge stone carved with strange symbols which indicated a huge treasure was located another 40 feet down. But then the pit flooded and they weren't able to go any further. Some people think pirates dug the pit and buried their loot. My money's on the Knights Templar, though. You can bet your boots the Holy Grail is down there."

You had to admire Griner. He always kept his ear to the ground.

"Where is Oak Island?"

"Canada. Don't you have cable?"

"No."

"I don't expect you'll be able to get it now that you're quitting your job."

The desk telephone rang.

"Parks department, this is Griner."

Griner's eyes narrowed as he listened.

"I don't give a shit," he said finally. "Cook whatever. I'll be there when I get there."

He hung up the receiver without another word. He disliked speaking with his wife.

"You know I can't give you a job recommendation. It's policy."

"I know."

Griner knew city policies backwards and forwards. He was sharp that way. He rose from gravedigger to parks manager in less than ten years.

On the way out Swiveller ran into Greta Bulkoch, his immediate supervisor. He'd hoped to avoid her on his last day but there she was, her presence looming in the doorway like a dark thunderhead.

"Gaspar took his lunch here at the shop yesterday," she said, frowning and puffing away at her small cigar.

"So?"

"So?" Greta's nostrils flared as she angrily exhaled a foul-smelling cloud of smoke. "He's supposed to take his lunch out on the route."

"I'm aware of that."

"Well, he's been showing up here at the shop and taking his lunch. It's starting to piss me off."

"Why? He always works hard and he's reliable. That's the main thing. How often does he do it?"

"I don't know. Every few weeks. Maybe more. What does it matter how often? Rules are rules."

"You do realize this is my last day."

"Yes, and you can do your job on your last day."

Swiveller shrugged and nodded his assent. Technically it was Greta's job to counsel employees on rule infractions. Delegating responsibility, however, was her forte. Besides, it was usually best to avoid any unnecessary interaction with Greta Bulkoch.

"By the way, Mel and I fired Dill yesterday."

"I heard."

"That will teach him to go over my head." Greta's expression became animated, like that of a grinning skull.

"Yes, I imagine it will."

Jimmy Dill was on his third year as a seasonal employee when Bulkoch made some sort of bumbling clerical error which resulted in Dill being reduced from 40 to 8 hours a week for the rest of the year. Dill made an appointment with Griner to discuss the matter. Griner admitted that Bulkoch had made an egregious error but said that fact was irrelevant since city policy stated the city does not guarantee employment to seasonal employees. Some mumbo jumbo along those lines. Indignant, Dill took the matter downtown to city hall. Once Griner and Bulkoch got wind of that, they immediately assembled a list of Dill's past policy infractions and terminated him within the hour.

Finally out of the office, Swiveller could breathe freely. Empty of people, the parks were quiet, frozen wastelands. The same snow had been on the ground for weeks. Though stretches of virgin whiteness remained, much of the snow was trampled into filthy, treacherous ice. Haphazard lines and swirls of yellow and orange dog piss decorated the snow banks and outcroppings creating strange images like those sometimes imagined in clouds or Rorschach inkblots. Swiveller saw cave paintings—stick warriors in elaborate beaded costumes carrying shields and throwing spears at other stick warriors in similar garb. A urine saturated sphere of snow the size of a soccer ball glowed yellow in the surrounding blue-white like a dying star.

Trudging through Arcadia Park Swiveller came upon Fern Stone-Jones defecating into the snow a few yards from the picnic site where she and Roy Flowers kept house.

"What are you doing?"

"You're like a stuck record, Clyde," replied Fern, hunched over next to a young cherry tree, her face pinched in annoyance. "Always the same questions, the answers to which are stupidly obvious."

"Okay. Here's another. Why don't you use the restroom like other people?"

"I'm not other people," replied Fern. The mist of her breath rose and swirled in the frosty air. "When you're young, taking a shit is no big deal. Once you get old it's the devil's own business."

According to street legend, Fern Stone-Jones was once a celebrated artistic gymnast. She made the papers after a good showing at the P&G Gymnastics Championship in Eugene, Oregon in 1975 and would have won the gold on the balance beam in Montreal at the 1976 Olympic summer games had not Nadia Comâneci spiked Fern's Gatorade with Old Grand Dad or something.

In any case, whatever agility, coordination, strength and poise she may have possessed was long gone. Once she finished her business it was all she could do to rise from a squatting position—but she finally managed by grasping the handles of her walker. She paused momentarily to catch her breath and then bent over to pull up her soiled panties and jeans. A rime of faeces adhered to the reddened and infected cheeks of her ass, which she didn't bother to wipe off. Her hide was tough and knotted, like the rear end of a chimpanzee.

"She's doing the best she can, Clyde" said Roy. He lifted himself slightly from the bench, narrowed his eyes into tiny black dots and farted. "It's too hard for her to get over to the shitter with that walker of hers."

"I realize that. Still, there has to be a better way."

"There isn't," replied Fern. "Rope me a cocktail, Roy."

She zipped her fly, and gripping the walker, scooted over to her usual blackened seat at the picnic table. She plopped herself down. Roy obediently got up and ambled over to the creek. He pulled a can of 211 from the swift icy current and tossed it to Fern. With one hand she made motions in the air as if she were trying to rope a calf with a lariat and with the other she tried to catch the beer. She missed. The silver 24-ounce can hit her in the chest with a thud.

"Goddamn it, Roy. You're really starting to piss me off. Now my cocktail is all shook up. You're always shaking up my goddamn cocktail. 20 years and nothing changes."

"Oh, and with you something changes? Why don't you hush for once?"

Roy picked absently at one of the dozens of cigarette butts frozen to the picnic table. Stuffing protruded from the shoulder seam of his canvas jacket. He was now completely toothless and the stubble on his grizzled face was pure white, with the exception of his moustache, which had a yellow tint. Both he and Fern had grown old and feeble seemingly overnight. Perhaps a year before they had begun referring to Swiveller as Clyde. It was as if they no longer recognized him, as if the daily skirmishes and turf battles of the previous years—all of which Swiveller admittedly lost—had never happened. The end was near, he was sure of that.

"What's with the straw?"

Six or seven bales of straw sat around the perimeter of the picnic site. A few had broken open, scattering over the snow and ice.

"It's not straw, it's hay," said Roy. "Some goat ropers from

Oregon had a cowboy wedding party over at the shelter and used the hay for decoration. It was a lucky find."

"How do you they were from Oregon?"

"Their pickups all had Oregon plates."

Swiveller pulled a few dried, golden yellow stalks from one of the bales. "This is straw, not hay."

"Don't give me that shit," said Roy sourly. "I know my hay. My grandpa had a farm. I spent the summers there when I was a kid. Best days of my life. Smell that fresh air. And notice how quiet it is. You can't hear any traffic. That's the hay, man. Hay is heaven on earth."

"Hay is dreams," added Fern. She tipped her canned cocktail and swallowed half the contents in one gulp. She set the can down, closed her eyes and breathed slowly and deeply as the soothing alcohol coursed through her body.

"What does that mean?"

Fern opened her eyes and belched. "Use your imagination."

The day was indeed beginning to feel like a dream, thought Swiveller. Though he knew it to be true, it didn't seem real that he would not have to hassle with the straw, that he would never again have to haul away their daily accumulations of refuse and junk or inadvertently step in one of Fern's turds.

"Looks like you guys are all ready for Christmas."

A few battered Christmas ornaments and a length of silver and gold garland hung from the snow-covered lower branches of the Sequoia tree. Nearby stood a three-tiered snowman with sticks for arms and cigarette butts for facial features.

"Roy's always trying to Feng shui the place." Fern rolled her eyes and lit a cigarette. "Next he'll be gluing wall paper to the trees."

"Just trying to make things festive," said Roy. "You never know when it will be your last Christmas."

"I suppose I should tidy up here a bit," said Swiveller, surveying the litter of beer cans, cigarette butts and discarded adult diapers scattered about the picnic site.

"We'll clean it up," said Fern.

"You always say that. But since it is my last day at this job, I'll take you at your word."

"Last day?" Roy looked up. "Are you retiring?"

"No. Quitting."

"You're quitting a city job? That's dumb."

"Probably so."

Fern beckoned to Swiveller to come closer. She whispered in his ear. Her breath was horrible.

"If anything happens to me, Clyde, don't let him get away with it."

"Who?"

"Roy. There's good and evil in this world. Roy is evil for the sake of being evil. He likes it."

"Alright," said Swiveller.

Fern had been accusing Roy of trying to kill her for years. In fact, the first time Swiveller met Fern she was going on about some ex-boyfriend who had stolen her bicycle and was intent on disembowelling her with a sharp butcher's knife the next time they met. It wasn't five minutes later that said ex-boyfriend rolled up on her bicycle and the two immediately began kissing passionately and cooing to each other. It was Roy, naturally.

The cell phone in Swiveller's pocket vibrated. It was Greta Bulkoch. There was a citizen complaint about some sort of mess at the archery range. No other details. When it came to citizen complaints, you never knew what to expect. It could be anything from major vandalism to a discarded gum wrapper.

Swiveller took his time and arrived at the archery range some 45 minutes later. He opened the gate of the chain-link fence and carefully made his way down the steep icy path. Midway down, he noticed a red and gold gym bag that appeared to have been tossed in over the fence. The bag had opened on impact, spilling brightly colored objects out on to the path. Reaching the objects, he discovered they were sex toys: dildos, butt plugs, several bottles of lubricants with exotic sounding names and a repulsive, squishy piece of rubber molded to resemble female genitals. The bizarre object featured a vagina, pink colored labia and a little puckered anus. What appeared to be faecal matter adhered to one toy—a rubber dildo in the shape of a penis complete with veins and a set of wrinkly testicles. Swiveller shook his head and headed back up the slope for a square point shovel.

Once everything was scooped into a large plastic garbage bag, Swiveller emerged from the archery range for what he knew would be the last time. He tossed the loot into the back of the truck and stood motionless with his eyes closed, feeling the soft pings of tiny snowflakes on his face. It seemed fitting that all he had to show for his years with the parks department was a collection of soiled sex toys. He laughed to himself as he imagined the treasure hunters at Oak Island, after centuries of digging, finding not the Holy Grail, but the 18th century equivalent of a bag full of dildos.

Opening his eyes, Swiveller saw the faint twinkling of the downtown Christmas lights. The starless cloudy skies were growing darker as dusk approached. He slowly breathed the fresh cold air. It tingled in his lungs and radiated a strange energy throughout his entire body. The sensation was deeply, incredibly gratifying. He continued to breathe in and out. For some reason, he imagined himself breathing for the dead. Surely the dead remembered how wonderful it felt just to breathe on a crisp winter evening. Swiveller was grateful he was alive to do it for them. It seemed somehow necessary. It was a kind of Kaddish

Boise, Idaho
2007-2015